GW00381705

Hazel Grove

The Dark Marquis

Black Velvet Books
Coronet Press

~

Copyright © Francine Howarth 2019

All characters in this book are fictitious.
Any resemblance to real persons is purely coincidental:
whether alive or dead

~

Real persons and places of note are featured.

~

All rights reserved. No part of this publication may be
reproduced, stored in a retrieval system, or transmitted in
any form, or by means electronic, mechanical,
photocopying, recording or otherwise, without prior consent
of the author.

Author Note:

Dear Reader,

~

The City of Bath and real-time houses situated in the surrounding countryside are most definitely featured within this book, though the latter have been afforded fictitious names. As with any book in a series, many characters from book one reappear, and new characters add spice and daring to chill-laden scenes one expects to encounter within murder mysteries.

Very best Wishes
Francine.

Prologue

Hyde Park, London 1819: September 9th

Golden hue of dawn bathed the horizon as three riders emerged from the shadow of trees; their steeds as though ghostly apparitions walking on a silver sheen of mist.

The lead rider huddling beneath a greatcoat reined back, thus allowing the others to come abreast.

"I see 'em. A lantern be up ahead, yer lordship, and they've not spied us as yet."

The diffused glow readily guided them onward to the appointed place where the duel would commence; a cacophony of birdsong cloaking their clandestine advance.

What did it matter if the Marquis of Rantchester was about to risk all for the sake of a woman? Never had he fallen for a woman in the manner he had fallen for Estelle, and the damnable challenge had come as no great surprise albeit several hours after an incident outside *White's* Coffee House.

But how like an army officer who deemed insult toward a young woman as of no consequence, and then sore vexed at an aristocrat bettering him in the tactics more akin to a street ruffian. True enough the officer was caught off guard, for his opponent had in the heat of the moment broken with convention of officers and gentlemen conducting their differences in private. Indeed, the fracas in a public place had left the officer smarting in more ways than one.

Far from best pleased at having to rise and dress at such an ungodly hour of the morn had served only to heighten Rantchester's own determination to teach said officer a lesson he wouldn't forget. Savouring a sudden light breeze

1

shimmying through the leaves whispering ever onward dragging the mist into the dark depth of the trees, its swirling nature matched his restless eagerness to be done with the sordid task ahead.

Intent on keeping his favoured horse well away from the close-quarter action of duelling and inevitable report of pistols fired across the glade, he turned to his groom. "This is far enough, Jem."

The last thing he wanted was for young Huntsman to lose confidence now that he was coming along nicely under saddle. And so, at his command all three riders reined their mounts to a halt; a deep toned voice carrying toward them on the shifting ether.

"About time, your lordship," said his opponent's second, followed by a mild taunt. "Tis nigh past the agreed hour of engagement."

"Give Rantchester some latitude for getting here before sun up," said the very man, whose insult to a lady had incited a fist to his foul mouth a day past.

There was no denying it was the Captain's right to demand satisfaction, albeit too dazed at the time of the incident when his red-coated arse landed in the dirt at the lady's feet. But here was Finch once again baiting trouble.

"Damn it all," said Finch, snide in tone. "The marquis here can barely get his cock up before noon after a night of pipe dreaming, and the thing is, his fancy piece do like an early riser." The captain laughed. His boldness in goading amounted not only to that of impressing his entourage, it was a purposely aimed insult to rile his opponent into a rash response and a hoped for badly aimed shot mid duel. "And 'tis a bold and confident man who chooses to arrive by saddle."

Rantchester dismounted keeping his thoughts to himself as to why he had chosen to come on horseback instead of by carriage, as might be needed if the duel proved fatal for his part. Likewise Edwin Lord Brockenbury said not a word as he too dismounted his horse.

Jem remained in the saddle and handed down the boxed pistols to his master's second. In turn Lord Brockenbury passed the reins of his horse into Jem's care, and said for their ears only. "Pray to God, Georgette never gets to hear of this."

"She'll not if my shot is true this morn," rallied Rantchester, handing the reins of his horse to Jem's hand. "Finch will have wagered my aim will be off through lack of practise now that I am no longer a man of military brass. Believe it, Edwin, Finch and his cohorts will be far from boasting of this come the morrow. I know my pistols, and the breeze is barely noticeable. I'll not miss my target, and if all goes well he'll not raise another pistol with his right hand."

Edwin glanced at the box containing duelling pistols, braced his shoulders and then strode forth to meet with his counterpart, Lieutenant Connors.

Whilst watching his lordship hastening onward, Rantchester removed his greatcoat and slung it over the withers of Jem's horse, "Right then, the sooner it's done the sooner we can all indulge a hearty breakfast."

Long shadows were lessening across the green swathe as Rantchester began treading Edwin's path, though movement near to the carriage at a short distance and beyond his quarry drew his attention. There was at least one other person standing in the shadows beside the carriage, the man's red tunic partially obscured by a dark cape; the driver atop and groom keeping the horses steadied.

Far from immune to the reality he might by fluke of misfortune meet his maker on this fine morn, Rantchester prayed for a quick end should death be his sorry lot.

3

Captain Finch bowed in military manner heels clicked together. "I had quite thought a marquis would choose to die by the blade."

Rantchester chuckled. "Ah, so you wish to up the stakes with a duel to the death."

"Now look here," said Lieutenant Connors, "it was agreed a wounding would suffice."

"You heard, the marquis," said the captain, the two military red tunics stark in contrast to Edwin's dour black greatcoat. "I'll not argue with his preference for a speedy death. As it is, pistols suit me better."

Edwin spun round, expression of incredulity, and his grey eyes glittering like diamonds. "I cannot agree to any dual to the death enacted before my eyes."

"Come now," said Finch. "We're all soldiers here."

"There you are wrong," said Edwin, his tone grave. "And this dual will proceed as agreed beforehand."

"On your say so, alone?" challenged Finch, furthering in snide manner. "A mere second setting precedence on rules of engagement already decided upon. I think not. As it is, Rantchester wouldn't want it any other way. If he didn't know it outside *White's*, he knows now that he made a fool of himself over a two-bit trollop."

"He's a man of legal silks, nonetheless," said Rantchester in reference to Edwin's status as lawyer and judge of the realm. He was damned if he'd to rise to Finch's bait. A level head was needed for what must be done and besides, his pistol would speak for him, all in good time. "Best you play fair, Finch, or the judge here will decide your fate."

Finch laughed, and addressed Edwin. "Very well, then, and when I am done with your marquis, *lawman*, I trust you'll have the stomach to tend to his wound. It will be severe, no doubting that."

4

Connors stepped forward. "Gentlemen, may we proceed?"

"Indeed," rallied Rantchester.

"The lantern marks the spot," said Connors, striding forth, the avenging duellist and Edwin trailing in his wake. "We are agreed eleven paces, turn, aim, and fire, on command, are we not?"

"Yes, yes," said Finch, exasperation evident.

"Captain Finch, *Sir*," said Connors, taking up position opposite to Edwin, "it is for you to choose your pistol first, from the aggressor's box, albeit you are the aggrieved. You nonetheless challenged him to a duel, and pistols are his chosen weapon."

"Cease your bloody rambling, Connors. This is far from my first duel, as you well know." Edwin opened the box and for a moment Finch seemed a tad becalmed, as though unsure which pistol to select. His hand hovered from one to the other. He then made his choice fleet of hand as he checked the pistol to be sure it was loaded. "Let's get this over with or the park will be overrun with early morning riders and we'll have ourselves an audience."

Rantchester reached for the remaining pistol, stepped back a pace and presented his back to Finch, Finch likewise.

Connors removed the lantern, and he and Edwin backed up ten paces. When safely out of line of fire, Connors, said, "Gentlemen, are you ready?"

They were and in unison responded.

"Eleven paces," stated Connors.

As the strides were called aloud Rantchester concentrated his mind on the vital moment of *aim*, *fire*, for he harboured no illusions to the fact Finch had it in mind to kill him. The distance covered was exactly eleven paces and on command he halted and awaited the command to turn. It came forth from Connor loud and clear, but as he turned a shot echoed across the parkland and pain seared through his shoulder.

Damn it to hell, Finch had fired off mark. The bastard had flagrantly disregarded the honour of facing one's opponent instead of shooting a man in the back. Despite severe pain in his right shoulder, despite a darkened patch spreading across his finely tailored blue coat Rantchester turned to face Finch: thanking God he was left-handed. They had one shot, one chance of each wounding or killing the other. Finch had cheated. Finch would now suffer the consequences.

Edwin's statuesque figure seemed as though frozen, his expression declaring shock and disbelief. Finch on the other hand was standing looking aghast. He was now defenceless, and for Rantchester it was infinitely satisfying to aim the pistol directly between the captain's eyes, but, whilst truing the aim downward for a disabling upper elbow shot as prior intended, another shot rang out across the parkland. Finch faltered in step and then slowly his knees gave way and he fell to the ground.

Rantchester let fall his pistol, for the soldier in the shadows had fired the shot, and with speed and dexterity the Lieutenant relieved Finch of the duelling pistol. "Get on your way, gentlemen. He's dead," informed Connors, the pistol thus hurriedly handed to Edwin. "We never met this morn."

"But we have a dead man, for God's sake," said Edwin.

"We cannot just walk away."

"You can, sir, and you must. We'll see to Finch, and you'll hear nothing more from us."

Connors turned as the man standing in the shadows came forth, his cape discarded and sergeant's stripes now evident. "This ain't the first time he's shot a man in the back," said the sergeant, "and we agreed if he were to do it again it would be the last time. He's a disgrace to the regiment, and that's a fact."

The carriage rolled forward, and Connors said, "Leave him to us. We know what we have to do?"

"And that is?" demanded Edwin.

"We'll have to think up a cock 'n' bull story for the commanding officer."

"Leave them to it, Edwin," said Rantchester. "Finch dishonoured them, the regiment and himself by default of cowardice when duelling."

"There is that, but he's dead nonetheless, and this whole damnable business goes against everything I stand for."

"Aye he's dead, and good riddance," said Connors aware Finch was being hefted unceremoniously into the carriage by the sergeant and groom. "Good day, gentlemen. We'll be on our way." Without further ado Connors stepped aboard and the carriage moved off.

Edwin's expression implied incredulity for a second time that very morn. "And we let them go, just like that? What happened was little short of murder."

"Indeed we do let them go, for I am bleeding in the manner of a stuck pig, and Finch is not worth a second thought."

"How bad is the wound?"

"I have no inclination to look for the moment, and best we get on our way as though we're merely out for an early morning ride. No sense in drawing attention to ourselves, so best you get off back to your house and by a differing route than Jem and I.

Jem drew alongside with the horses, and quick to dismount wasted no time in helping his master re-don his greatcoat in order to hide his bleeding wound, and equal in haste at getting his master to saddle.

Edwin handed the pistol box to Jem, and whilst mounting his own horse directed his attention to Rantchester. "I'll take the circuitous route back to my abode, and you can then cut straight back through the trees. "I'll see you next at Monkton Heights, for I am off back to the country this very afternoon. You must come for dinner as soon as you've settled Estelle at Hazel Grove, and bring her with you. Georgette will be pleased to see her, be assured of that."

Without further ado Edwin set off at the trot, and Rantchester turned to Jem. "Right then, back the way we came. I'm famished, and this damnable wound is bloody painful."

One

Upper Belgrave Street: London: September 9th

It was but nine of morn.

Indeed, a thoroughly indecent hour of the day to come calling on a marquis, more especially one renowned for falling into bed in the early hours.

The doorbell clanging in the hallway implied sense of desperation by the person on the other end of the bell-pull. Whomever, he would know soon enough. Though he was damned if he was going to abandon his breakfast, not even if the Regent himself was standing below stairs.

Head thudding from excess of wine in vain hope of lessening conscious awareness to pain in his shoulder, how glad he was the doorbell suddenly ceased its tiresome irritation. Clearly a footman had finally taken the necessary steps, and the visitor would soon be left to await the master's presence in the lower salon. But such was not to be, for a well-known voice boomed loud and clear, his footfalls ascending the staircase purposeful in manner.

"The dining room, you say? Right." The door was suddenly flung wide, and the ruggedly handsome face before him was that of a man incensed and about to say his piece.

A London newspaper thrust forward under Rantchester's nose shrouded kidneys, bacon, scrambled eggs, coffee and just about every damn thing he was about to attack with zest, post duel.

"You damned fool, Rupert", said his father, mouth almost curling in the manner of a rabid dog. "If you dare to marry that woman, so help me, I shall, by abrogate, have your inheritance rescinded and bestow it upon my sister's first born son; merely the title yours."

And the Marquis of Rantchester remained seated in mere momentary defiance to the presence of his father, the Duke of Leighdon. As it was any quick movement might cause his wound to reopen and a scarlet stain spreading across his shirt would reveal evidence of injury to his shoulder.

Despite his father's hand shaking with rage it afforded time to peruse the newspaper headline:

Marquis Involved in Fracas.

Well that was it then, Estelle was now known to his father.

"Outside *White's* of all places, a more public place you could not have chosen. And by God, had the injured man pressed charges against you, think of the scandal in that."

Knowing his place in the scheme all things the aristocracy he finally pushed back his chair and gained his feet, infinitely glad his father had no knowledge of the duel nor the circumstances of his opponent's death.

His father's imposing height and demeanour erred severity, his discerning scrutiny of son with unbuttoned shirt minus cravat implied his offspring was less than worthy of the family title and the shame of his aristocratic loins. Nevertheless they were long since well matched in adulthood and he was no longer the child living in fear of his father's vile moods. And he would not have his father refer to Estelle as '*that woman*'.

"Estelle is of good blood, albeit several generations removed from the family earldom."

"Whatever possessed you to get entangled with a mere colonel's daughter of common blood and of all things, brawling with another over this damnable woman?" His father shook the newspaper, clearly despairing shameful evidence of a marquis applying his fists to another in public.

One bushy blond brow suddenly arced in distaste, as his father furthered with, "Heaven's above you're a marquis, and you'll wed nothing less than aristocratic bloodlines. Do you hear me? I expect a lady of rank and title to bear the heir to the Leighdon fortune. Furthermore, this scandalous article refers to your drawing a blade and states the other man suffered injuries. Is that true?"

"I drew in self-defence."

For a moment his father looked as though he might self-combust. "Over a damned woman, a woman who entertains men at will."

"Estelle has kept me sane this past year, and I'll not wed that mare-faced loopy you favour as the front-runner."

"If not Isobel Lady Mayberry, then I shall arrange for another to fulfil the task of providing the requisite heir. You've had thirty years of life and I'll have no more of your bucking the issue of marriage. Has it not occurred to you my time is limited on this earth and I wish to see evidence of a grandson before I depart to the nether world? I had thought your playing the filly field in sporting manner would have waned by now."

"It has, and Estelle will make for a good and attentive wife. She has my heart, or at least, as much as I am able to give her besides my love of equines."

His father laughed. "Let her keep your heart, and you hers if you must, but you cannot wed *that woman*. Wed the Lady Isobel, get her plumped with the requisite heir and keep your mistress or some other. Is that not a fair deal?"

11

Was he hearing his father correctly? This was the man who alluded to impeccable moral standing and always looked down upon men tempted by the flesh of young beauties. God how he thanked his mother's bloodlines for his general facial appearance, for his father's rugged features had begun losing the handsomeness that had turned many ladies heads in his direction and now served to announce him as an aged patriarch of eight and fifty years.

"What is so wrong in marrying a woman one feels great affection for? Estelle is of reasonable blood, a beauty to boot."

"Then find love with a true lady, and rid yourself of that harpy. Damn it all, Rupert, she's a woman of renown who dutifully serviced several gentlemen before you went a calling at her Bloomsbury salons."

Damn his father. Damn his birthright. Damn the whole bloody establishment. Thoughts of wedlock to the Lady Isobel chilled his blood. Nonetheless, to appease his father was sensible for the present."

"All right, I shall consider the Lady Isobel."

"Good, that's settled then."

It was far from settled, and the path ahead could become rocky in the next week or so, for Estelle was at that very moment travelling from London to Bath ahead of him and would arrive there a day hence. Although reticent about taking up residence at a county abode, she had eventually given sway to his desire for her companionship beyond the confines of London. Although not ideal, separate residences for the present were agreed upon in lessening the chances of their being spied together, and he was sure Estelle would soon fall in love with the house acquired on her behalf.

His father again intruded on his thoughts; voice commanding full attention. "I shall have your mother send invitation to the Earl of Mayberry, and suggest he and his good lady wife should come dine with us at Huish Downham, all in timely manner." A smile for some apparent reason creased his father's face, but momentary. "Avail yourself this week to thoughts of marriage, for if nothing else the admirably suited Isobel has a fine body and by all accounts is much charmed by your lean handsomeness. Although of no great beauty you'll couple nicely enough no doubt. Damn it all, Rupert, if you cannot abide the look of the girl, cast her night chemise over her head and the deed will come easily enough. A betrothal will be broached as soon as considered appropriate over a glass of brandy." His father turned on his heels, business clearly concluded. He then paused, mid stride, their chestnut brown eyes colliding: the only element of likeness they shared. "Keep your mistress out of sight and should she fall with child you will not, under any circumstances, accept liability. Do you understand what I am saying?"

"I understand perfectly well, though cannot and will never deny my responsibility for a child of my blood."

"Then on your head may fall the anguish of an affronted wife, for if a mistress becomes known to your lady wife your domestic situation may well be rendered intolerable. Women are an intuitive species and readily sniff out deceit as well as a cat smells a rat, and any illegitimates you sire will forever be the brunt of their scorn and bitter recriminations."

He almost cheered his father for his observation of women in general, and then it occurred to him his father was perhaps not as honest and upstanding in moral behaviour as he would have others believe.

On reflection there were many times in the past when his father had arrived home later than expected. And, occasions when he had taken unexpected last minute business trips, of which had prevented mother accompanying him on said ventures. Happen there was more to his father than met the casual eye. Hence the cool affection displayed between his grace and his duchess in public and utter lack of affection in either direction when in private. Not that it mattered all that much, for he had felt estranged from both parents throughout his entire and memorable life, when not in a drunken stupor or opium induced haze.

"Did you hear a word uttered, Rupert, or are you under the influence of damnable opium?"

Insolence became him when it suited, and such suited now. "Perchance your *Grace* was forced to cast aside a mistress for the sake of propriety, thus you are hardened in heart."

The sound of silence fell akin to a hammer blow to a black void between them, until his father rallied with a noticeable twitch to left side of mouth. "A man of the world has many a cross to bear in his lifetime, and this is but one that lies across your path and needs placing to one side."

Ha, his father could jut his jaw all he liked in feigned empathy, whilst his eyes bore the mark of deceit.

"Did you marry my mother for love?"

"I did. Does that please you? She however, married me out of obligation to her father's wishes. And there lies the rub of a woman who fulfils her duty to both men and thence becomes as good as a corpse in one's bed. I had no mistress at that time, though I cannot deny I have sought the company of such from time to time over the years."

"What of your first wife, the mother of my half sisters?"

"I married her out of obligation to my father's wishes, she likewise. Nevertheless we became friends and as you well know Charlotte passed on shortly after giving birth to Hattie."

"And your grace expects me to hurt Estelle whose kindness deserves respect, and then to wed another just to conform to what is expected of a future duke?"

"Quite so, and no more to be said, m' boy. I shall send word prompt upon reply from the Earl of Mayberry. Your presence will then be expected at Huish Downham. Good day, Rupert."

There was no brooking argument with his father, but he could not bend to his elder's wishes. It was too late to step away from the commitment he was now bound to uphold. He glanced down at his own reflection within the mirrored sheen of the dining table. Damn his father, damn him to hell and back.

Upon the sound of the duke having vacated the room and the door having closed, frustration and anger caused him to fist the polished surface of the dining table with force. Silverware bounced, fine bone china rattled, and breakfast no longer held appeal. He back-swiped his coffee cup clean from the table, and for all but a second out of time the sound of shattering china proved infinitely satisfying, but damnably inconvenient to his need for coffee to sate enraged thirst. Nonetheless, his butler appeared on cue with flat-pan expression.

"Will there be anything else, your lordship?"

"Yes, a cup and more coffee. Hot strong, and black as night. And send word for the Huntsman to be out front at noon on the dot. I shall be away to Bath directly."

Two

Monkton Heights: September 15th

Edwin Lord Brockenbury laughed in hearty manner. When at home his lordship was carefree in spirit and far removed from his dour persona of hard-nosed lawyer and learned judge. "Good Lord, Rupert. So he has no notion you are . . .?"

"None whatsoever."

"You're not— not about to be faced with a breach of promise suit?"

"Not if I can avoid it."

"Then pay visit to Huish Downham and get it over with," said his lordship, uncrossing his legs as though about to leap from his chair, though he merely shuffled forward in seat.

"Easy for you to say."

Edwin shrugged. "What alternative is there?"

"Pen a letter and set off for a grand tour of Italy."

"The coward's way out? I never thought to hear that from you, not after our soirée in Hyde Park." Edwin immediately reached across to a drum table set at a handy distance betwixt the chairs, and rapidly assessed the level of port in a crystal decanter. It was somewhat depleted since their settling to discourse within the library. "Another drop before coffee?" he enquired, and promptly reached sideways to tug at a bell-pull beside the fireplace. "It ceases to amaze me the number of arranged marriages that have fallen foul to breach of promise suits in recent months alone."

"Of which my father has threatened will occur should I renege on a formal contract of betrothal witnessed by Isobel's parents."

"Yes, but the agreement is yet to be signed by all parties, is that not so?"

Rantchester swigged the last of his port. "Two days hence."

"Then the sooner the truth is out there, the better."

"The duke has threatened to ban me from all property owned by him, should I fail to show up for a very private dinner party, the sealing of the deal party. Hence, my present dilemma."

Edwin raised the decanter and poured to the glasses. "A young man of title rebelled a month or so back after having dallied with an actress. He went to the altar on special licence and has since faced disinheritance."

"Yes, but once the scandal of it all slips from the forefront of gossip with the matriarchs of the *haut ton*, the happy couple will again show face, as did your beautiful lady wife."

A fleeting hint of discomfort streaked across Edwin's darkly handsome features, as though a moment of disquiet from his past had leapt to the fore. "Georgette had nothing to answer for. She was wholly innocent and became the victim of vindictive tittle-tattle."

Coffee arrived on a silver tray and thank God the butler's intrusion stole Edwin's attention, otherwise silence might well have hung heavy for a moment or two. It suddenly occurred to Rantchester that his reference to Georgette as a *'beautiful wife'* had somewhat rattled Brockenbury, though for why escaped him.

Damn it all, he himself had once adored Georgette and asked her to marry him. Part in jest and part in earnest, and

18

had she said yes he would have been wholly surprised albeit the happiest man alive at that time. She hadn't though, and he hadn't really expected her to. Edwin on the other hand had won Georgette's heart from the moment they first encountered one another, so what had his lordship recalled that set him so ill at ease?

Georgette Lady Brockenbury giggled.

Seated on a chaise opposite to her lady guest, she clasped her hands together and drawing her forefingers to her lips in amused pose, said, "He must have realised, surely, how awkward it would be to simply let his father hear rumours of your relationship. I feel sure with the right approach Rupert could have garnered the duke's alliance. After all, your beloved is wholly conversant with London society, and the duke is really not an ogre at all. He is one of the most charming men I have met next to his son."

"Precisely, and the upper echelons of the *haut ton* will not look kindly upon me, for I hail from the lower military element of society; a mere colonel's daughter. How can I possibly reveal the truth of my past? Though I fear that is of little consequence now, and Rupert has enough to contend with in pondering how best to approach his father and reveal his intentions."

"And once confessed to it cannot be *undone*," said her ladyship, a tentative smile. "That much is assured, and Rupert has never looked happier."

"I would like to think so. However, the prospect of introduction to the duke and duchess fills me with dread."

"If not for you Estelle, there is no telling how far Rupert may have travelled the dark path he was treading before you came into his life. Nor can I, in all honesty, believe the duke has remained ignorant to his son's past indulgences. As for what you have told me about yourself," continued her ladyship, casting a compassionate sense of understanding by way of eye contact, "you merely had gentlemen officer friends, and for a young widow such friendships are far from unusual when a sadly departed husband's fellow officers rally to the cause of a grieving widow."

"Perhaps not, but I did however live alone with few servants and entertained without a chaperone, thus many officers wives considered it a shameless business. I lost many friends because of surmised wanton behaviour for my part."

Her ladyship laughed, amusement etched on her face. "Oh dear, I must apologise for that unseemly outburst, but female tongues do wag with gossip and sometimes very hurtful if accusations of impropriety are falsely exaggerated."

"Indeed, their accusations were false in account of unseemly dalliance with Captain Finch, though correct in respect of a gentleman of whom the wives were thankfully unaware of. They had by then ceased keeping or wanting my company."

"I see, so you did have an acquaintance with the young officer prior to the incident outside *White's*?"

"It was but a fleeting flirtation and amounted to nothing meaningful."

"And the gentleman, the one the ladies knew nothing of?"

"At first I thought it might lead to a worthwhile arrangement, and in some respects it did, but not as I had imagined or hoped for."

"I take it you were fond of the gentleman, perhaps in love?"

Dare she reveal the truth fully to a close friend of Rupert's?

"Although the past is in the past, on reflection, yes, I did fall a little in love with a man whom I knew in my heart could never fully commit to me in the way I desired of him."

"And along came Rupert to the rescue of a broken heart."

"I am not sure it happened in quite that manner, for he lied upon our first meeting and if not for the Captain's outlandish behaviour outside of *White's*, the fact Rupert was indeed a marquis came as quite a surprise. For after a year of knowing him I ask myself how did he keep that from me, but of course as merely his mistress he paid visit to my house and I none the wiser. We travelled about a great deal, and always to isolated places far removed from society, and elements of his life I still find difficult to understand. I am not absolutely sure he has abandoned the evils of opium, for there are times when his eyes seem strangely unseeing. And there are times when I feel his heart dwells elsewhere."

"Do excuse my unladylike behaviour." Her ladyship turned slightly and raised her dainty feet to the chaise and settled herself with one arm to the claret-coloured velvet bolster. "I feel so ungainly at present, and heat of summer drains every ounce of energy by eventide."

Estelle sensed her ladyship's action as purposeful in manner and Rupert was no longer the desired subject of discussion. "Do you not take rest of an afternoon?"

"When alone, yes, but when Edwin is here I relish his company. I no longer travel to London with him, or any place that involves a journey of more than one hour."

"I would imagine a late summer baby is preferable to one born during the depths of winter."

"Do not believe that old tale. I much preferred Julian's confinement. It was December and it was so much easier to wrap up warm when necessary." Her ladyship shrugged in a most delightful expression of relaxed sophistication. "In all decency, and hot as summer has been I dared not discard too many layers, though I confess this simple gown has been utter Heaven. And with a wrap it still serves purpose on lovely days."

"It's so very pretty." Indeed her ladyship's gown was the envy of her guest, for the gown was of the finest white satin patterned with sprigs of lavender topped by tiny lavender blue bows edging the neckline. The very fact it was generously gathered at the front, albeit her ladyship's delicate condition and confinement close at hand, to the casual eye passed unseen, she looked the epitome of fashionable elegance. "It is so rude to enquire after a lady's seamstress, but might I ask who created such a lovely garment?"

"I confess I am most fortunate in having acquired a very talented young woman, whose needlework skills came to light quite by accident."

"Indeed, for I envy her masterpiece. Is it too much to hope her services are available within in the locale of Bath?"

"There are very capable seamstresses and haberdashery establishments within the city. Mrs. Paltry of Milsom Street served me well enough when I first settled at Hazel Grove. However, whilst my butler began his acquisition of new household staff, a young woman arrived on the doorstep with samples of her work. Of which she displayed with dolls in fashionable dress, a delightful sight in themselves. A very good judge of a person's skills Taylor took it upon himself to engage her on the proviso of at least one recommendation proffered and easily verified. Well, as it turned out her previous position was that of seamstress to an aged lady, sadly deceased, and confirmed by none other than the lady's lawyer. Needless to say my darling husband being well acquainted with said lawyer sealed her position within my household and, when we came here, Poppy came, too."

"Oh I see, and a fortunate encounter for Poppy."

Her ladyship tilted her head forward eyebrows raised, a quirky smile flickering at the corner of her lips. "I could suggest Poppy might like to return to Hazel Grove for a month and again engage her talents in creation of fashionable garments to your liking and needs at present."

"But will you not require her services for when . . . when the baby is to its cradle?"

"By then you will have no doubt procured a seamstress."

"Should things go badly between Rupert and the duke we may not be able to afford the rental on Hazel Grove for more than a few months, and I may have to seek a modest abode in keeping with my allowance from my father's late estate."

"I am of mind the duke will blow hot in the first instance of receiving Rupert's news, and will then settle to the realisation that his son's happiness is more important than high-minded belief a title must wed a title."

"But you have?"

"Circumstance caused Edwin's elevation to his father's title. After all he was third in line to the Brockenbury Estate when I set eyes on him for a second time, and I think I knew that day, or shortly afterwards that I would wed him if he asked for my hand. As for the rent monies on Hazel Grove, should Rupert's father embark on all that he has threatened; your marquis is nonetheless a rich man in his own right."

"I swear I had no notion he was a marquis until the day outside *White's* when we were both accosted by Captain Finch, who jibed in vociferous manner at Rupert for taking a woman below his rank."

"I understand Rupert felled the man and justly so, by all accounts." Her ladyship cast a smile. "Was it the same officer who caused concern beforehand?"

"It was, and a very frightening incident in itself."

"Frightening? Were you attacked?"

"Oh no, Captain Finch and I just so happened upon one another in St James's Park. He reined his horse to a halt to pass the time of day in his usual crude manner, and I chose to ignore him. In spite he urged me out of his way, and before I could clear the path the animal caught my shoulder a passing blow. I then tripped over my own skirts and stumbled. As it happened Rupert was not too far distant taking a drive in his carriage and spied my mishap. His groom leapt from the carriage and rushed to my aid; the carriage thence beside me. Rupert and I fell into discourse and he insisted on seeing me safe home, and declared himself to be that of Rupert Bathampton. I had no reason to believe otherwise at that time and although it was inappropriate to accept his offer to ride in the carriage without a chaperone, I was a little shaken and bruised and we *were* accompanied by a coachman and groom up front so I saw no reason to refuse."

Her ladyship raised a fine white pearl-encrusted lace fan to her face and waved it in rapid manner. "And what did he claim as his occupation?"

"Lawyer, and I had no reason to think he was fibbing."

"Indeed, how wicked of him."

"He paid visit at my abode the very next day to see if I had quite recovered, and I think that's when I realised his intentions were not altogether honourable."

24

"The incident at *White's* . . . was it as bad as reported in the newspapers? And thank the Lord the army officer's injuries were minor."

"Luckily there were more than adequate witnesses to declare Captain Finch attempted to draw his sword when it became obvious Rupert was besting him with fists. In some respects it is a good thing Rupert keeps a dagger strapped to his boot, and he was so adept at placing the blade to the captain's throat whilst flat on his back at my feet, the fracas immediately ceased to be. Needless to say, Finch was so dazed it required the services of two fellow officers to heft him up and part carry part drag him away."

Her ladyship shivered merely for effect she supposed, for heat within the room was quite oppressive despite garden doors cast wide. "Let us hope nothing untoward arises from the incident, for it was foolhardy of Rupert to engage in such an unseemly manner." Hurriedly lowering her feet to the floor, her ladyship said, "Shall we take a short turn about the terrace?"

They did just that and a gentle breeze cooled the flesh in pleasant manner, and whilst standing surveying the view from Monkton Heights in silent repose, her ladyship's attention quickly drifted to the partially constructed gardens dropping away below them.

"The terraces as you can see are looking a little sparse in places," explained her ladyship, pointing at paved paths and levelled bare earth in readiness for planting. "Where the steps lead down from each terrace I have it in mind for gloriously romantic urns to be placed as sentinels either side. The second terrace I thought might be rather nice if planted with roses and surrounded by lavender hedging. The lower terrace fronting the grass, I think lends itself to a vast herbaceous border."

"It all sounds perfectly lovely, and to have a lake as well, is wonderful."

"Yes, I do rather love strolling by the lake, and to have a pavilion at the far end near the trees would be marvellous. Can you imagine taking tea by the lake?"

"I can, and I envy you this house. "Although her ladyship had plans and clearly loved the lakeside walk, Estelle sensed air of detachment as though the house and gardens might never be as loved as those at Hazel Grove. "It's breathtakingly beautiful, and when all is complete the joy you shall derive from having designed it yourself will no doubt compensate for not living at Hazel Grove." A glint of reflected light caught her attention. "Is there another house within the trees beyond the lake?"

"Yes. Monkton Abbeyfields. The greater part of the house was razed to the ground by fire. Edwin decided he would rather have a new house instead of rebuilding the old. He also had trees planted amidst existing ones to shield the burnt out shell from view."

"I won't ask why, because I sense it has a sad story attached," said she, for Rupert's rendition of several murders and the terrible event that led to the loss of the old house was frightening indeed, and she well understood Lord Brockenbury's desire to screen it from view with the help of woodland.

Her ladyship averted her gaze from the vista before them and asked, "Are you happy at Hazel Grove?"

"Very. The house is so pretty with its floral facia."

"I miss it so very much. I suppose that sounds incredibly selfish to grieve the loss of a relatively modest country house when we have this, but I so loved the honeysuckle, the rambling roses and ivy intertwining up and over windows and doors, and the heady scent of honeysuckle wafting into the house was utterly divine."

"Can you not have the same here?"

"I shall, eventually, though it will take the passing of many years before this house will equal Hazel Grove in my affections."

As her ladyship once again cast her eyes to the view, Estelle studied her profile. If ever another woman could launch a thousand ships as claimed of Helen of Troy, it would surely be Georgette Lady Brockenbury, for she was the fairest and most captivating beauty seen in a long while.

"We wondered where you were," said his lordship, drawing their attention whilst making forward to his wife's side.

Rupert remained in the doorway shoulder casual to doorframe drinking the sights before him as though what lay ahead mattered little to him, but it could not be that simple to let his inheritance slip from his grasp. He suddenly caught her eye, a smile creasing his handsome face as he heaved himself upright and raked fingers through tussled blond hair.

"Tomorrow," he said, striding toward her, "it has to be done by tomorrow."

This was the man who with the mere touch of his hand had quietened a terrified filly hell-bent on killing an ostler with her hooves, and yet, hours later had placed a knife to a man's throat as though about to slit it open, his expression murderous. How would he fare tomorrow, and how might he react if his worst fears were realised?

Three

Huish Downham: September 16th.

His heart drummed, and although he was seated with his back to the horses the house was as real in mind as that of the stone structure standing proud at the end of the sweeping drive. With each turn of the carriage wheels grinding on gravel, they were now descending the gentle slope from the main gates.

The rhythmic beat of four-in-hand pounding the ground at the trot; the carriage began drawing them into the imposing fold of Huish Downham.

Sitting opposite with eyes to the fore keening the path ahead, Estelle's expression implied sense of awe and trepidation. "It has a beautiful setting," said she, casting eyes from side to side as the carriage traversed between iron-railed fencing and rumbled on beneath the avenue of trees stretching from the gate to the lower slopes. "Are these horse chestnut trees?"

He inclined his head to take in the view of several horses flicking tails across their flanks whilst idly savouring the shade of overhead green canopy. "Indeed they are."

Her voice as always fell as music to the mind, the very thing that had caught his attention, and led him to believe she was an actress on the day of their first encountering one another. His penchant for ladies of the stage had almost become his undoing on occasion of one declaring she was with child, for upon discovering by chance he was a marquis not merely an officer and gentleman, she set out to

29

ensnare him by writing to his father. Money changed hands he presumed for the girl vanished never to be seen again.

"I do so love trees and of course, their botanical names are oft fascinating," intoned Estelle, drawing him from reverie.

"Enlighten me."

A beautiful flush flooded her cheeks. "I feel sure you know as well as I the correct botanical name, *Aesculus hippocastanum*."

"I assure you I am the least educated all things botanical vernacular."

A shy smile swept to her heart-shaped face as though but a young girl putting forth to her elder and sensing it inappropriate. Her violet eyes ever inquisitive seemed to delight in meeting his gaze, for she was not the least bit shamed by the intimacy they shared in full.

"But the house, you must be able to tell me something of the house, for it is still part obscured from view."

"It was built in 1570 as a quadrangle with stable mews to the right with clock tower entrance. The south facing aspect to the casual eye appears somewhat severe. It nonetheless has a fine *porte cochère* entrance, which embodies sense of welcome to weary travellers. Oh, and the interior I feel sure will meet with your expectations. The state rooms are vast, light and airy."

"State rooms?"

He dared not laugh, for her expression implied terrified female wishing herself anywhere but on approach to his father's residence.

"I thought . . ."

Her hesitancy delighted him as it had on their first encounter, as had her vulnerability that day of his seeing her knocked off balance and left in the dirt by Captain

Finch. If he had to marry and beget children he hoped it would be with Estelle. Never had she made financial demands upon him as had his previous mistresses and she deserved his loyalty. He sensed her heart was wholly his, but he had a past and someone in that past had driven him to the dark side of physical gratification, and Estelle had indeed saved him from self-destruction.

"I had no notion the house would be so— so—"

"Ostentatious is the word, and it's a place to lose oneself in, literally." He chuckled. "I vaguely recall an incident as an infant when I lost my way, though cannot remember where exactly a footman discovered my errant backside. Thereafter hide 'n' seek became a game of derring-do and caused mayhem, with servants sometimes seeking my whereabouts for hours."

"You deliberately ran away and hid?"

"It was the only means at my disposal for drawing mother's attention, and the household staff played along with my ploy."

"You mean she neglected you?"

"Not intentionally. Her duty nonetheless entailed paying court to father, and my elder half sisters had no desire to have a boy at heel, nor of his poking his nose in their bedchambers. Seeing as how a boy is but a small man and no less curious of the female form than that of a randy adult, thus I oft strolled into their bedchambers unannounced."

Estelle blushed as though remembering the day of his standing close to her bedchamber whilst they were engaged in discourse and his asking was she terribly bruised from her encounter with an unruly horse. With the door left ajar, his taking advantage to sneak a peek whilst she removed her pelisse and changed her dirtied gown for fresh attire had proved irresistible. How well he recalled her cheeks flaring

31

as soon as spying his reflection in her dressing mirror. If not then, it was but a few moments later when she must have known for sure his interest in her was anything but innocent. Far from naïve as first imagined, and living alone with a few servants, it soon became apparent Estelle had indeed entertained gentlemen alone and without a chaperone in attendance. She conversed with ease and although flirtatious in tone she was far from coarse in mannerisms or dress as were many women of whom he had associated with in the past.

He had no doubt she would readily adopt the mantle of a marchioness with grace and style, and he didn't give a damn if his mother refused to meet with her except it might hurt Estelle, initially. It was his father he was wary of, for the duke would likely set out to pay her off and be rid of her. Such underhandedness could not be allowed to happen for he had to have an excuse to avoid betrothal to Isobel, and if it was thought he was already wed he was safe from that catastrophic end to his life.

"Oh my goodness, Rupert," said she, once again drawing him from reverie, "the house is vast."

"It is that, and perchance we shall arrive unseen by pater and mater."

"I fear my heart is at odds with my head, for although I know we must face them and allow them to share in our joyous news, I would have preferred that you had come alone in the first instance."

"We are as one and as good as wed, albeit we have not taken the final step to official wedlock," said he, reaching forward to cup her hand between his, "and where I go, you go." He drew her lace-gloved hand to his lips. "Should the duke prove difficult as he no doubt will to begin with, bear his scrutiny and hold his gaze. He cannot beggar our souls even if he chooses to sever my birthright cord. I shall declare us wed, and if need be we can with special licence fulfil the criteria in order to have paper declaration of our committal to one another."

"I cannot say I approve of our deceit in this matter."

He chuckled. "We have each other, you bear a ring upon your finger, and that is all that matters to us for the time being. It is no odds to anyone whether we are married or not."

The carriage began swinging to the left taking a wide sweeping turn, the house no longer at his back, for it now towered over them, drawing them into the *porte cochère*. Soon the horses were at a standstill, a footman in attendance at the carriage door. Two more footmen hurriedly stepped from the house and took up position either side of the main entrance doorway. The butler, she presumed, stepped forth in order to greet them or to send them on their way.

"Good morning, your lordship. His grace spied your carriage on approach and awaits your presence in the library."

With his back to Pettigrew whilst assisting Estelle in alighting from the carriage, Rantchester sensed the butler had something on his mind. Pettigrew then coughed in the manner of gaining attention. "It was suggested your lady friend might wish to remain in the carriage or take a stroll through the grounds."

"*Friend*, lady friend?" snapped Rupert, his stomach knotting as he turned to face Pettigrew, the lie slipping from his tongue with venomous intent. "The Marchioness of Rantchester, if you please."

Pettigrew's jaw dropped; mouth wide, bushy brows knitting together until the reality of Estelle's elevated position struck home. He then bowed in manner assuaging any sense of personal slight against Estelle. "M'lady, welcome to Huish Downham.

"Rupert," said she, stepping down, "I am most happy to take a turn around the grounds, whilst you and your father engage a moment alone."

"Five minutes no more," he conceded, determined he would not have his father ignore Estelle as though she were indeed a woman of ill repute, albeit she was a shameful hussy on occasion. As for *carte blanche* afforded to a manservant to think her less than a lady was nothing short of contemptible disregard for her feelings, and the hurt now inflicted upon her could not pass unchallenged. He would not have Estelle insulted in this manner, no matter his father's outrage at his bringing her to Huish Downham unannounced. "I can see myself to the library, Pettigrew. Be so good as to show my lady wife the way to the walled garden."

With that said he ascended the steps and strode directly to the library, his father as expected standing with back rigid to the vast stone hearth, lethal intent etched on his face.

"Your daring, Rupert, is beyond words. Did you think a duel at dawn and the death of a young officer would slip to the mists of time and no one any the wiser? You insult my intelligence if you are of mind I would not see the connection of a punch thrown outside *White's* and the death of your opponent; the very morning I called upon you. At the time I confess your taking an early breakfast seemed at odds with your previous bent to stay abed until noon. All I can say is thanks to the *Almighty,* for the perpetrator of the officer's demise remains unnamed in *The Herald* of two days past."

"Captain Finch died by the hand of a non-commissioned officer."

34

"The duel was nonetheless betwixt you and Finch. Am I correct in this?"

"You are, and I have a wound to the shoulder telling of Finch's cowardice in firing off point."

The duke's expression mellowed somewhat. "Cheated, eh? Then I have cause to thank the *Almighty* for your safe deliverance, though cannot understand your stance on defending the honour of *that* woman, whom you've dared to bring to my house. Surely, you did not suppose your mother would willingly receive your mistress and gladly sup tea with the likes of her kind."

"Her *kind*?" Rantchester chuckled, delighting in letting his father rant and rail, for soon the moment would come, the moment his father would explode and denounce his inheritance, and in all honesty he didn't give a flying pheasant for the lands of the dukedom. Estelle was his sanity when the convenience of dream smoke escaped him, and his hell-rake days were in the past, as was his commission: now sold. "If you were anyone but my father you would be flat on your backside for that remark."

"You think?" challenged the duke, a conceited smirk, "then it is time I revealed a little of my past triumphs as a boxer, something I indulged when at Harrow. There is more akin in nature between the pair of us than you realise, my boy. You asked me a few days past had I ever had to choose between true affection and that of duty, and the answer is yes. One can marry for love and fulfil one's duty only to discover love is a one-sided affair. Illicit affection thence sought and found elsewhere became an obsession of which I'm not proud by any means. Nonetheless, the thrill, the desire, the temptation of youth became detrimental to the very thing that meant everything to my existence and purpose in life. You were my greatest delight, my son, my heir, save excess desires of the flesh overruled my duty to your upbringing and I remained absent from Huish Downham far more than I should have. I bear regret, Rupert, and cannot undo what has passed between us in this matter of duty that I now wish you to abide by, as I had to."

"That I cannot do, for out there strolling in the rose garden is none other than my wife."

The duke sidled sideways, casting his eye through the window. "You damned fool, Rupert," said he, his expression strange indeed.

It was impossible to read his father, for the duke's eyes assessing the figure of Estelle in her gown of purple silk with lavender coloured velvet Spencer erred voyeuristic fascination. After all, her frill-trimmed parasol shading her face from the sun presented a pleasing backdrop to her lovely face. If it was anyone other than his father he would have deemed the elder attracted to her in unseemly manner.

Expecting further tirade of verbal abuse from his father, the duke turned with a sad expression. "Of all the people you had to fall in love with it had to be that vision of loveliness, and I know not what to say." His father slipped into the nearest chair, head to hands implying sense of utter despair. "Have her come inside. The sooner we sort this sorry business the better for all concerned."

Something in his father's words stirred disquiet, as Rantchester stepped to the bell-pull.

The duke rallied and regained his feet. "I'll not ask you to give her up. It's too late for that. However, you will not bring her here again, nor will the pair of you be invited to attend at family gatherings. I warned you against indulging your whim beyond keeping her as your mistress."

"If that be your wish, then so be it," batted Rantchester, defiant as ever.

Silence hung like a dark cloud, Rantchester unwilling to engage further, the elder again with his back to the hearth as though bracing himself against an invisible enemy. Pettigrew appeared prompt in response to his summons, the duke quick with issuing orders. "Fetch the young . . ." His father's hesitation was momentary, as though choking on his words. "Ask the marchioness to kindly present herself here in the library."

As Pettigrew retreated, the duke turned his attention back to the window. Again silence descended, until the door opened and closed with a gentle click. "I had no notion you were here, Rupert," A waft of rose water perfume drifted across the room, his mother's pale blue eyes levelling on the duke in accusatory manner, her beautiful face a little tainted by age but still arresting and her husky voice alluring. "Have I imposed upon a private matter of some import?"

"Not in the least," replied his father. "Our business is quite done with, and Rupert will see you to your chambers."

"I came merely to collect the book I chose earlier," said she, snatching at a small leather bound book discarded on a side table near the door. "Come Rupert, it seems we are both dismissed, and I have not set eyes on you in a long while. You must have news aplenty to keep me entertained for all of five minutes."

The bitter rebuke from his mother was expected, and the duke's dismissal his way of saying *get your mother out of here, now, before she sets eyes on Estelle.*

Rantchester had no alternative but to oblige his father and remove his mother post-haste.

As though reading reluctance in his body language, the duke said, "That other business I shall now have to conduct alone. Be assured I shall be kindness itself, and no bitter utterances."

If nothing else, his father's word was his bond and he clearly had no intention of upsetting Estelle. Rantchester caught up his mother's elbow, opened the door and ushered her from the library, hoping to hell they made it to the grand staircase before Pettigrew emerged through the garden door, en route with Estelle to the library.

Four

Fear cloaked about Estelle. The house was every bit as grand inside as that of its exterior. The panelled hallway she imagined could quite easily house a banquet, and yet its stark beauty was merely adorned with padded settles here and there. A suit of armour housed a corner, shields and crossed swords gracing the walls. A vast stone arched hearth drew the eye beyond that of a circular table centre hallway.

In passing onward her eyes were drawn to a grand oak staircase, which stopped at ten steps and there was another suit of armour as though a sentinel guarding two further stairways wending upward to a gallery arcing around the hall.

Far more interesting was the portrait-festooned gallery where a haze of faces looked down upon her whilst the butler led her from the hall to the library.

He stopped abruptly by double doors, knocked and waited, though the summons to enter came almost immediate of dropping his hand to the handle in readiness to open the door. Ushered inside, she expected to see Rupert, but there by the window eyes to the rose garden was a somewhat familiar figure. Disquieting shivers shimmied down her spine.

Oh God, was it possible?

As he turned her worst fears were realised, his voice almost a husky whisper as though fearful his butler might be eavesdropping. "Dear God, Estelle," said he, striding forth. "I swear I never wanted this, never imagined Rupert would disobey my wishes and bring you here."

Rendered speechless and heart in mouth, her hand taken in his afforded no option but to follow his lead to the far side of the library. Albeit a darkened corner, it was the worst moment in her life. Presumably safe from eavesdroppers and well away from the windows, he drew her lace-clad hand to his lips, his blond silver-tipped moustache tickling whilst applying a kiss to her fingers.

"This is a most embarrassing affair, Estelle, and I know not what to say."

She drew breath, steeling herself to reply. "Nor I, now that I know who you are, for I had quite thought you were Malcolm Uffington, gentleman landowner who came to town on occasion and took a fancy for a young widow. Now it all makes sense as to why you were always so vague about your place of residence, and why you had sought a lady companion to share the delights of modest entertainment to be found within the city. You and your son are liars both, and I utterly fooled by Malcolm Uffington and Rupert Bathampton."

A smile streaked his rugged features. "As I recall, you were not averse to my earnest attentions, and you seemed happy enough in paying visit to music halls and delighted in travelling by hansom cab. Had I arrived at your door in a carriage with a crest upon the door then my secret life with you would too readily have become common knowledge." He drew breath, a shuddering breath, his visage a picture of man remembering intimate moments. "Sadly, you are now married to my son, and believe it, our secret will remain secret. I have no wish to reveal the nature of our previous arrangement and thereby inflict misery upon Rupert, though I think my silence deserves a little reward in return."

"Reward?" Her heart dived her mind reeling in fear his intention might be to renew their acquaintance as before. "You cannot mean to—"

"Come now, Estelle, our former friendship cannot be cast aside and forgotten so readily."

"You cannot expect me to once again be your mistress, albeit in name only, for I cannot oblige your secret whim as I did before."

"Do not cast stones as though I failed to serve you as expected. Your inner desires were testament to the extent you would have gone to had I offered for your hand. Such could never be and albeit temptation led me close to damnation on many occasions of your wilful teasing I never fully broke with our rules of engagement. Believe it, Estelle, my support in the near future will become an asset to you."

"Does our previous friendship mean nothing to you?"

"It meant a great deal."

She could not step back to the life led before Rupert became a part of her life. "Then be my friend now and let bygones be bygones."

"I bestowed the wherewithal for a lifestyle beyond your means, the epitome of wealth and standing and asked very little in return." He laughed softly; deprecating laughter. "And by God, you'll become a duchess some day and all of this, albeit at my expense," said he gesturing to the roof over their heads

"I had thought that was nigh impossible."

"Oblige my greater knowledge all things expected of a future duchess and Rupert will inherit all that I have."

Her heart raced, her mind a jumble of fragmented memories, memories she had so desperately cast aside in wanting to forget her past life. "If I agree to your demands, how can I be sure you will honour your word?"

"Have I ever given you cause, cause to doubt my word before?"

"You have not, but it is all so different now."

"Estelle, my dearest girl, what I am asking is but a small price to pay in securing your future and my son's inheritance. There is much under this roof of which you are unaware, and I suspect Rupert has revealed little to do with his mother or that of the life led here at Huish Downham. Do you even know whom you have wed, what his passions are beyond sexual gratification?"

"I know that I love him for who he is not what he may inherit."

The duke laughed. "Then you are sadly more naive than I had thought possible, for my son has a dark side, a side to his nature that may well destroy any happiness you have garnered in the throes of initial heady marital euphoria. He and his mother are two of a kind, both prone to self-destruct when the slightest thing tips the balance of their shaky inner worlds."

There had to be escape from his threat, the innuendos, and some means of avoiding further engagement. "If you are trying to shake my faith in Rupert, you shall not succeed."

"Such could not be further from my mind, Estelle. Nonetheless, you will abide to my whim, and you will keep company with me as and when I deem to engage in your education of becoming a duchess."

"How, how are we to meet and no one any the wiser?"

"A portrait, you must sit for a portrait. After all, when you finally become the duchess and take up residence in this very house your portrait will adorn the upper gallery as do all the duchesses that have gone before."

Had he suddenly taken leave of his senses? "A portrait, but I thought—"

"You think too much, Estelle, your curiosity almost your undoing at one time." He chuckled. "Do you recall the day you enquired as to where my country abode might be and, that you thought it had to be in the West Country because my voice implied that was so?"

"I do recall that day, and I meant no harm by my inquisitiveness, for I thought we were well acquainted enough by then to venture to discourse on your life away from the city. However, your reluctance and immediate change of subject I took as warning that you had a life you preferred kept private. It was the day the thought came to mind that you probably had a wife and children and that I had been squarely duped by a thoroughly uncaring person."

"Far from uncaring, Estelle, for I grew overtly fond of you, and had I no commitment to a wife at that time I would have sought to take our arrangement beyond that of mere companionship and voyeuristic pleasure. As you rightly say, circumstances have now changed, and reinstatement of our previous arrangement will not impede your life at Hazel Grove, nor will it interfere with your life as wife to my son."

"What you are asking of me is tantamount to betrayal, my marriage thus meaningless if I agree to your demands."

"I warned Rupert of the consequences should he dare think of marriage with yourself." The duke ran fingers through his hair, frustration evident as though unsure how to proceed. "Damn it, you will both rue the day of his mother discovering the truth. That alone will be a traumatic experience, not only for Rupert but for you as well. There will come the time when you will seek my company and counsel, and to that aim of establishing a plausible reason for sense of friendship betwixt you and I, it is to young Ranulph Brockenbury that I seek the perfect excuse for discreet encounters. He has a very capable apprentice who excels with miniatures, and two life-size portraits of late have gained young Harper much approval from ladies of the *ton*. I propose you commission young Harper to paint your portrait, a full portrait and a miniature, for I know Ranulph is run ragged with commissions for the foreseeable future. Sittings for a portrait will necessitate regular visits to the city, thus providing the perfect solution for innocent encounters. Be assured you will come to appreciate my support."

"And where are these innocent encounters to take place?"

"I have several abodes in Bath, and Harper will not mind where he fulfils his commission, so long as he garners regular payments for visits to his favoured tavern."

"I cannot believe I am agreeing to such blatant abuse of Rupert's trust, but I fear I have no choice."

"Precisely. You married my son, and once the truth is made known to the duchess she will be incensed and as like will demand Rupert's rite to inherit the dukedom be rescinded until such time as your marriage is either annulled or divorce initiated and concluded. If you refuse to accept one or other of my proposed outcomes; the land and all will go to my nephew." He reached out and trailed a finger from the tip of her chin to throat and thence to shadowed cleft invitingly enhanced by the diamond pendant he had given her long ago. "You see, it is not so terrible to let a man indulge his voyeuristic fancies. After all, it is a perfectly enjoyable pastime to savour the visual delights of the female form."

She understood perfectly well she had no choice but to obey his demands, the manifestation of his engorged manliness quite evident within his breeches. It pained her to think she had at one time delighted in that response from him; his innocent pleasure taken in exchange and no physical demands expected of her. His gifts likewise had amounted to wholesome array of gowns, jewels and beautiful items of great worth, as much her means of attracting a wealthy suitor as that of pleasing him when he chose to pay visit.

"It could be said you took advantage of a young widow lacking in skills suited to employment, whose late departed husband's pension and a father's inheritance served only to pay rent on my Bloomsbury salon and modest living. It was, perhaps, wrong of me to give sway to your seeking paid companionship, and I should never have answered your advertisement."

"I remember that day oh so well, and your nervousness as you strolled along the embankment." He chuckled. "You were the prettiest picture, all in pink and rare innocence about you, and I wanted then to bestow beautiful jewels and glorious gowns upon you."

Indeed you did, and your generosity proved beneficial in provision of dining in grand if discreet manner at private establishments, trips to music halls and small theatres, and other venues I could not otherwise have afforded."

"And I appreciated your company, and would have continued to do so, had you not sent that missive to my club declaring our arrangement at end and no explanation. Did you really think I would not call at your abode on receiving your dismissal?"

"If you did; my maid said not a word of your having stopped by."

"That's the thing; I refrained from stepping to your doorstep upon spying my son's carriage at the door, and duly ordered my hired hansom cab onward, and prayed Rupert's fanciful interest in your pretty little hide would rapidly wane as it had with all his previous fancies. How foolish of me to have thought of you as a naive young widow and happy with your lot and that of my little lady friend, when you were but seeking a husband of rank and means you had become accustomed to on my generosity."

Rupert too had thought her enchantingly naïve, but she had indeed set out to ensnare him from the moment his carriage had drawn level and their eyes had met. Her accidental brush with a horse, although genuine enough, she had used to her benefit, and had not realised at the time but had fallen romantically in love with her gallant.

"There was never love between you and I," said she, unwilling to concede any nuance of affection toward him, though had indeed grown very fond of him, perhaps more than was sensible. "It was merely an adult arrangement."

"I confess mild affection grew to something more substantial for my part. And as I said beforehand, there were times when temptation almost led me to break with our agreement; times when I wanted far more than merely indulging the occasional intimate caress."

She dared not say there were oft times she had wished he might ask for more, her body crying out for him, aching to be loved with fullness of man. Always, always the difference in their ages had played a part in keeping their acquaintance as a business arrangement. All along she had sensed an affair of the heart would have led nowhere, and despite his rugged handsomeness he was more than twice her life years. That of which they had once shared was in the past, her heart now Rupert's.

"And our agreement this time entails nothing more than voyeuristic pleasure, and that you will keep your distance?"

"On my honour, and tea taken between married kin is not a crime," said he, bowing whilst catching up her hand and again placing a kiss to her fingers. "The miniature will be mine. Agreed?"

She could not deny they had shared in happy times, and although Rupert's handsomeness was immediate to the eye at first glance, his stance was less imposing than his father's Greek god persona, but she loved Rupert, loved his lean muscular frame which cut-a-dash no matter his dress, and his smile enduring and endearing.

"Agreed, but I cannot say I am obliging your whim in good spirit."

"I had not thought you would. Nevertheless I shall reimburse all expenses incurred in the commission of both portraits. That is, should Rupert be less than favourable to your sitting for a portrait. Now, there is however one rather unpleasant matter in need of clarification. You will not be invited to Huish Downham in the near future. Any notion of such presented to Rupert's mother, for the moment, will cause unnecessary disharmony within these walls. Given time she may mellow, though in all honesty such is most unlikely if she continues in her present frame of mind."

"It is no hardship to me, and I shall not hold it against her. It is the way of life, for social standing has its limitations as to who can and cannot step across class boundaries."

His face embodied sense of compassion, his eyes embracing her assets, his words again inciting inner disquiet. "Now that we are reacquainted the prospect of your paying visit here would have pleased in extremes, alas I must make do with secret liaisons." He then turned avoiding eye contact for guilt of intent glittered in his eyes. "I have something I wish you to see." He strode toward a desk, and there opened the uppermost drawer. "This is the handiwork of young Harper. Beautiful, don't you think?"

She must hold her fear in check and not let him sense the panic welling within, for she really did not want to relive aspects of her past life. She nonetheless moved to stand beside him, for he was holding forth a miniature portrait set within a rather ornate gilt oval frame.

"Oh very beautiful, and who is this?" she said, stunned by the lady's slightly provocative pose.

47

"I have no idea. Harper was desperate for money."

"I see why you keep it hidden."

"I know not who the lady is for sure, and cannot justify its presence out of the drawer." The door to the library opened with gusto as Rupert appeared. "Ah, my boy, what do you think to this miniature? It's merely a suggestion, but do you not think a portrait of your wife is called for?"

Rupert's face expressed confusion, though given the seeming congeniality of two people studying a miniature portrait it must have been the least expected scene he had thought to encounter. She could only pray he would never discover the extent of her previous acquaintance with his father, nor that he should learn of his father's hold over her. She had to oblige in order to protect his inheritance.

Her supposed husband stepped close, faint essence of sandalwood causing a ripple of pleasure to eddy down her spine, as he tilted his head to view the miniature, and exclaimed, "Good God, that's Freddie's wife."

"Struth," exclaimed the duke. "Not young Rose Davenport? Good Lord. It is. I see the likeness now. Then what in the deuce was young Harper doing in selling this?"

"Ranulph's apprentice *sold* it to you?"

"I thought it damn strange at the time, his sidling up to me outside Sally Lunn's and then offering a pretty face for sale." The duke glanced her way. "Never mind what I thought he had in mind for sale until he thrust the miniature under my nose. He was quite adamant a client had commissioned it and then couldn't afford to pay for it. Nevertheless the quality of his work stole my eye."

"But to sell a miniature of Rose dressed in that pose, his employer's sister-in-law at that. Do you suppose he paints lewd miniatures of all the ladies who sit for portraits?"

"If commissioned to do so, I shouldn't wonder. A husband or lover might wish to be in possession of such a delight."

"Freddie's prone to bouts of secret gambling, and it could well be he was lacking the wherewithal to cover the fee for the miniature."

Listening to the two of them mulling the finances of one man whilst deliberating over whether the other had acted with honourable intent or not, seemed trivial to the fact a woman in scant clothing, albeit a portrait, had fallen into the hands of anyone willing to purchase a salacious image.

She moved to stand by the window, her own fate that of a miniature destined for the duke's hand a tad unnerving. Pray to Heaven Rupert would never know of its existence. Their departing from Huish Downham could not come soon enough, and she was not in the least sorry she would not be paying visit again: not for a long while.

Five

Hazel Grove: 8 p.m.

Something was wrong with Estelle. And whilst watching her standing by the window, clearly lost in thought, if asked why he had felt uneasy at finding her and his father seemingly engaged in pleasant discourse that very morning, he could neither explain nor fully understand it. The happy atmosphere had seemed at odds with his father's former stance on *'that woman'* as a most unsuitable wife for a marquis. It was hard to believe his beloved had won his father over in the short time of his escorting his mother aloft to her suite of rooms, and yet it appeared as though Estelle had indeed gained sense of admiration and induced convivial spirit within the duke.

Perhaps he was letting his imagination run wild, for something his mother had said in passing had set him to thinking his prior action was thoroughly inadvisable at having lied to his father about his and Estelle's so-called marriage. It seemed his mother despised Isobel and thought her a most inadequate specimen for a future duchess, and had as good as told his father in no uncertain terms she would not entertain Isobel's parents in hope of securing a contract of betrothal. His mother had further said *'if you have any sense you would do well to marry uncontaminated aristocratic blood, for cousins continually marrying cousins has brought many families to the brink of inherited madness'*.

He had meant to raise that particular issue with the duke to ascertain what in the devil his mother had meant by her outburst, but the distraction caused by the miniature portrait

51

had thrown him off kilter and stolen the moment. Far from shocked by the lewd miniature of Rose Davenport, it was not unreasonable to suppose Freddie had commissioned it. He was a lusty fellow and given to great admiration of lewd sketches.

The memory of Estelle escaping to stand by the library window in similar pose to her present detached stance, had seemed natural enough at the time, but it seemed a damnably odd thing now they were well away from Huish Downham. What woman wouldn't be a little embarrassed by the image of another whose assets were barely covered, but there was something else about her reaction that hadn't rung true. Prior to his arrival she was entirely engrossed in the miniature, and he was not so sure he had read the situation between his father and his supposed bride as clearly as first thought.

Swirling brandy around and around in his goblet, his head spinning, he continued puzzling Estelle's withdrawal en route from Huish Downham albeit interspersed with prompts from him and exchange of momentary discourse. But damn it all, upon arrival back at Hazel Grove she had retreated aloft to nurse a severe head pain. Forced to partake of luncheon alone he had then ridden out to pass an hour or more engaging a woodland ride and a gallop on the downs, and upon his return still no Estelle. She had finally deigned to appear for dinner, and again any notion of pleasant discourse had proved nigh impossible.

Studying the way her arms were crossed and fingers toying the fine lace trim of her sleeves, her lithe frame draped in lemon yellow silk implied sense of stress, and he spoke his thoughts. "Hardly a word has passed your lips since our departing from Huish Downham, and you can deny it all you want, but I'm of mind our banishment from there has upset you far more than you care to admit."

52

Without turning, her response erred cold. "I know my place, be assured of that."

"And that would be, given my father seemed utterly smitten by your charming self."

"Smitten?" snapped she, spinning on her heels, anger and anguish evident. "He made it quite clear your mother is unlikely to accept my presence at Huish Downham in her lifetime."

"And that matters?"

"Of course it matters. Think of the children we may beget. What are they to think of a grandmother who will refuse to accept they exist?"

"I confess I am at a loss as to father's sudden approval of our supposed wedded bliss, and God knows how you won him over but you clearly achieved what I had hoped might happen. What man could deny you? I've oft asked myself the very same, and today you proved me right in my thinking."

"You dared to wager my feelings in a mad gamble that I might win your father over and thereby secure your inheritance, not giving a thought to the fact your mother will think me unsuitable as a future duchess. You never told me your mother would be against me. You've always claimed your father would prove difficult."

He swigged his brandy in one gulp, placed the glass to an occasional table and gained his feet. "Come here, and let us savour the triumph of your having won my father as your champion. To have him on our side is a victory in itself. As for mother, well . . . let me say this, she is not the dragon he would have you believe. You'll see I am right, all in good time."

"Then why—?" Her hesitancy erred confusion, her expression that of disbelief. "Why did your father insist it was because of her that I am not welcome at Huish Downham?"

He stepped closer, half expecting rebuttal given Estelle's tetchiness. "It's his way, for it is he who swore that if I married you he would indeed rescind my rite to inherit the dukedom which is not entailed with the title. As yet mother is ignorant to our relationship, and because of her delicate disposition it is imperative all be revealed at the right time in the right manner."

"I had no notion your mother was ill," said she, allowing his arms to enfold her. "Why did you not say . . . set me right on such matters?"

"Because although she is hale and hearty, mother suffers from temporary lapses of memory, an affliction that sadly befell her after a serious riding accident. There are days when she quite believes the duke is her father, and days when I have paid visit and she thought me her brother. At other times she knows exactly where she is and who is present in her company."

Drawing Estelle close, he savoured her slender form crushed hard against him, her beautiful violet eyes questioning his sudden and affectionate gesture as though it might be a trap she could not escape from if such became her wont."

"And today, how was your mother, today?"

Cupping her chin, forcing her lips upward in readiness to devour, he replied, "As a matter of fact, she was lucid, quite lucid."

"Then was it not a good moment to mention my presence?"

Tired of discourse on *why this, why not that*, his lips embraced hers, his intention to merely distract and the silence afforded him the pleasure of touch, caress, and to devour at will. Her response although sweetly accepting of his

54

dominant stance it was far from her usual willingness to engage in sparring with tongues and desire to caress in like manner.

Damn it all, her silk gown clinging to her contours had instilled a fire within. *Why not, why could he not have her there, in the sitting room?*

This new Estelle, the supposed marchioness was thinking herself too grand to indulge her lover's whims at will, when before today she would have slid to his lap teasing and inciting his ardour in playful manner.

Sensing reluctance for her part he pulled back and ceased their intimacy. "I fear you are not best pleased with me for some reason."

"It is not you. The blame is entirely mine, for I simply cannot shake off this pained head."

Convinced the pained head was little more than excuse to rid her of unwanted attentions, he said, "Then my love, you must away to your bed."

"Would you mind terribly much if I do?"

"Not at all," said he, leaning forward to kiss her brow. "I shall retreat to my town house for a couple of nights. I have business in town tomorrow afternoon. I shall then drop by Ranulph Brockenbury's studio first thing, and will return here on the Saturday."

"It's past eight Rupert. You cannot ride the highway at night."

"You need rest, Estelle. The journey from London to here; you claimed as tiresome. Settling to this house you declared as vexing, because you were unable to find things you wished immediately to hand, and your encounter with my father has greatly taken a toll as well."

"Rupert, please don't go, for I sense that I have now upset you."

"Not at all," said he, the lie tumbling off his tongue as easily as the lie told to his father.

"Stay, please stay with me this night." She reached for his hand and purposeful in placing his palm to the upper swell of her breast, she furthered with, "be patient with me."

Patience was one thing. To be denied the pleasure of her flesh whilst laid abed with her would be utter purgatory. "All right, I shall stay in the bedchamber next to yours."

"But why, when there is no reason for us to sleep apart?"

She would soon learn that to shun a lover had its downside. "As yet we are not wed, so in some respects that in itself is reason enough for separate bedchambers. Besides, sleeping in separate chambers has it uses."

"I cannot think why, but if you'll excuse me, I shall take my leave and retire to bed."

A kiss to his cheek sealed his fate of a cold bed, and as she departed the room he could think of many reasons for favouring separate chambers and in time Estelle would also learn to leave her old way of life behind and embrace the new, though to say as much would likely hurt her feelings.

Albeit aware of her previous lifestyle, he had no right to assume he could simply demand she abide to his whims. Nor had he any notion to jealousy of men who had bestowed gifts upon her in the past, for he was well aware her meagre funds could not have provided the wherewithal for her substantial wardrobe, and likewise his own generosity at times could have been construed as little more than payment for services rendered. How many lovers had stepped through her door beforehand had no bearing on his initial interest in her, for he was no better at that time than any one of them in seeking her favour. Her boldness despite feigned shyness had revealed much about her, and she most certainly had an eye for gentlemen wearing diamond pins to their cravats.

As the door closed quietly, he mused over the fact she now belonged to him, and it seemed as though she would indeed become his duchess some day. True enough, she had much to learn, not least how a marquis and a duke pass their time when not indulging the delight of bedding a compliant wife, or that of a mistress. He had no desire for the present in seeking a mistress and perhaps never would, and God forbid Estelle should ever feel the need for discreet encounters of a lustful nature. His own appetite in matters of the flesh he wagered would keep her faithful to him alone.

He had thought by having some sense of love as the foundation to a marriage it was the answer to a man's prayers. And to secure a wife of equal propensity for hedonistic bedchamber romps negated need for the risqué business of acquiring a said mistress, a distraction his father had finally confessed to. To have assumed for years there was someone other than his mother in the duke's life was a reasonable enough guess, for his parents had rarely indulged in mutual engagement and neither to his knowledge had shared a bedchamber in so long he could not even recall when last he had seen his father looking remotely as though having just stepped from the marital bed. Nor had he witnessed his mother with flushed complexion and downcast eyes in wont to conceal shameless behaviour. They did indeed lead entirely separate existences with exception of shared mealtimes, strained family gatherings and dinner parties.

He reached for the crystal decanter and the rich amber hue of Brandy. As the liquor swilled from its silver-topped vessel to crystal goblet, he almost laughed, for the nation England had warred with and, twice defeated the devil incarnate, was the very country Englishmen looked to for the warming tang of nectar fit for the gods.

Raising his glass, he said, "To Bony, a god of his time who met with godless Englishmen."

He duly downed a half glass in one, kept hold of it, grabbed the decanter turned and made toward the door. Early night it was, then, and come the morrow happen Estelle's pained head would have taken flight and all would be well in the loving stakes. If not . . . there were plenty of activities to keep him occupied. The first day of the hunting season was nigh, and his father's pack when baying in earnest was a bloodcurdling sound that echoed through moss laden woodland.

Six

Brock Street: Bath.

Bedlam seemingly prevailed in the Brockenbury household.

A giggling infant preceded Ranulph Brockenbury in greeting his visitor, though upon sighting his quarry the young rascal came to an abrupt halt; uncertainty etched on his cherubic face.

Ranulph hastened into the salon; his awkward stance of twisted spine pronounced, though no deterrent in sweeping the infant off his feet and tucking him under his arm. "I apologise for the intrusion of my son, your Grace, and shall have him removed directly."

Whilst struggling to retain grip on the infant, now wriggling with intent, Ranulph made toward a bell-pull. He need not have bothered because his wife came rushing in, her face flushed. And in like to her son she stopped abruptly as though her husband's visitor was indeed a frightening image of horned head and forked tail.

"Your Grace," said she, a sweeping curtsy performed with elegant flourish, "it is a great honour you pay us this day." Suddenly aware the child's bright blue eyes were staring up at him in questioning manner; she turned her attention to her son. "Wolfie, you are a wilful mite. You know full well you must not step beyond the parlour door when a guest is present."

The Duke of Leighdon he was, but there was no call for young Beatrice and Ranulph to feel in any way intimidated by him, and the last thing he wanted was for the child to think him some fairytale ogre. "Do not banish the child on my account, for I merely dropped by to offer premises that

59

may well prove convenient and timely." Already aware Beatrice was with child, he also knew lack of rooms had become a bone of private contention, and such had failed to escape Harper's hearing. "I have it on good authority that your apprentice has for several days set about seeking new and affordable lodgings to no avail."

Ranulph sought support from a buttoned-back chair, his hand heavily engaged with the polished wooden trim, evidence his spine still plagued and pained during prolonged periods on his feet. "I know not how you became acquainted with our domestic arrangements, and I'll not dispute this house has its limitations in provision of bedchambers." He ruffled his son's copper curls, very definitely inherited from Beatrice as was the infant's features. "As some might say, more children dwell here than adults."

It was not a visiting duke's place to mention the obvious that Ranulph's physical impediment bore no reflection on his virility. "I am aware your studio has become somewhat cramped with two portraitists in residence, and I had it in mind you might appreciate young Harper having a space all his own. If that is so, then I can assist in this matter, for I have modest cottages near the weir and one at present is lying vacant. I say modest, for although on three levels the cottage has merely a kitchen and parlour at ground level, scullery and cellar below. The upper level has two rooms. Above however, a spacious double attic with window to front and rear that is not only light but spacious."

Ranulph lowered his son to the floor, and whilst passing him to the care of his mother's hand, enquired, "And the tenancy would entail?"

"A modest weekly rental, which I feel sure young Harper will have no difficulty in raising from revenue gained by his own hand."

60

"That would be grand, my love," intoned Beatrice, a hand gentle in touch to Ranulph's. "His sleeping and working elsewhere would ease our situation greatly, and he can still share in our mealtimes and attend upon you for tuition."

Ranulph chuckled. "Harper has established his own mark, and much of his work is beyond equal to my efforts. He has the measure of light in ways I have never attained, and I am the first to acclaim his prowess all things preparatory sketches before he even dreams of applying colour to palette."

Beatrice cast her eye to the wall above the mantel. "How can you say that, Ranulph? People stand here and say that if they reach up to my portrait they are sure the silk of my gown will feel real to the touch."

"You are biased, *B*, and I love you for your supportive prompts. Nonetheless, it is high time Harper set out to establish himself in his own right."

"Perhaps, but I fear he will attempt to garner the favour of your clientele."

"And I would be happy and content with fewer commissions and thereby more time afforded for you and I and the children to escape Bath. Perhaps we could do the grand tour and partake of several months in Italy. Would that not be a wonderful adventure for all of us?" Ranulph raised his hand to silence any response from Beatrice. He then addressed the offer as presented. "If your grace pleases, we accept your proposal as a fine outcome, and shall pay due rentals for two months on the cottage, thus affording Harper time enough to engage commissions and thereby accumulate sufficient monies to see him able to cover future costs and ready himself for independent living."

"In that too I can lessen your burden in monetary matters, for in lieu of three-months rent a commission will come his way and two completed portraits will then be his rent duly paid in full. Thence onward he must cover his own expenses. Now, shall I approach the young man and set forth this golden opportunity for his due consideration, or would you prefer to announce my proposition yourselves?"

"It is your proposal and a very generous one at that," replied Ranulph, air of relief about him as though unburdened with a distasteful if necessary upcoming task. "It seems only right and proper to let you pass on the good tidings to Harper."

"Then might I have a quiet word with him?"

"Indeed, your Grace," said Beatrice, ushering her son toward the door. "Come Wolfie."

The infant swung round and beamed a smile and said, "Good bye, Sir Grace."

Amused at the infant's *Sir Grace*, he could not let the little chap go without a kindly response. "And, good day to you, *Master* Brockenbury."

As Beatrice closed the door Ranulph gestured to a seat beside the hearth devoid of laid fire. Instead of twigs and coal a riot of roses in shades ranging from the palest to the deepest of pink were standing proud in a vase, the whole now drawing the eye, the gentle waft of their scented blooms as pleasing as rose scented water on the warm flesh of a woman, though to visualise Estelle was dangerous indeed. Such thoughts stirred inner desires albeit the very reason he was there in Ranulph's abode.

Accepting his host's offer he settled to the chair, thus affording Ranulph the opportunity to do likewise. Ranulph refrained, his stance hesitant and indicative of a man with something plaguing his mind, though rapidly revealed.

"Does your offer to assist Harper have anything to do with a portrait commissioned this very morning by the Marquis of Rantchester?"

"My son, eh? Well, well. So he's finally decided a new portrait is called for."

"As I cannot accommodate any commissions at the present time I suggested Harper as an alternative portraitist, and your son agreed his work met with approval."

"Ah, and you suspect duplicity afoot, is that not so?" Ranulph looked affronted, and yet it was a reasonable enough assumption. "I assure you, dear fellow, your plight of small house, young children and a lodger came to my ears by chance. And, at that precise moment the solution to your problem happened to be staring me in the face and so I came directly."

"Then I am most grateful to your Grace, and Harper will no doubt present the marquis with a grand portrait of his future wife. That I am sure of."

Future wife, did Ranulph say future wife?

There was a light tap at the door. Presumably Harper had arrived hot-foot from the studio above stairs. How would he take to the offer of a cottage, if at all?

Besides, a burning question required an answer and the sooner the better. Thus the interview would be short and to the point, but the sweet essence of rose perfume lingered, taunting with memories of Estelle. The interaction betwixt Ranulph and Harper passed him by until Ranulph said, "I shall leave his grace to explain fully the details of his proposition."

Hazel Grove.

The house felt empty, and taking tea alone at four of afternoon was a little disheartening.

The truth being Estelle had not thought Rupert would leave so early that morn, and no note left declaring when he would return seemed pointed indeed. Had she offended him that much in departing for bed earlier than usual and wishing to be left alone the night prior? Surely not, for her head had genuinely pained in extreme. Not even a fusion of feverfew had lessened the misery of its persistence. In the end laudanum had served purpose and sleep had finally embraced, soothing away the strain of tangled emotions his father had instilled within her.

She had thought herself immune to any nuance of affection once afforded to the man she had known as Malcolm Uffington, until— until— No, she must not think of the duke, must not step back into the memories of shared laughter, shared moments of intimacy. She would soon be the Marchioness of Rantchester, and she did love Rupert, madly, though perhaps not as passionate as he might have imagined, at first. After all, she had set out to ensnare him. It would be folly indeed to let love slip her grasp, and what good would come from a parting of the ways?

Life could not have dealt her a worse blow than to discover her future father-in-law was the very man she had dreamed of wedding some day, his age immaterial, his presence once the only thing she had craved, until . . . Not that she had ever told him he was her Achilles heel, and yet perhaps he had known that all along.

She sipped at her tea the bell clanging in the hall denoting a visitor had come to call. It would be terribly impolite to turn whomever away. Nonetheless she wished it possible to retreat on occasions such as this, when her thoughts were so muddled. Perhaps it was the local parson for he had said he would call of an afternoon and no

64

definite day or time as a guide to his hours for paying visit to parishioners.

All but a few minutes and a knock at the door preceded Dora the maid. "A gentleman, to see you ma'am," said she, casting the door wide to allow entry to the Duke of Leighdon.

Estelle's heart stalled, the cup toppled from her hand and crashed to its saucer, a silver spoon in turn catapulted across a silver tray colliding with a sugar bowl mid flight, and tea cascaded down her afternoon gown.

Dora rushed forth to relieve her mistress of the upturned cup and saucer, and duly handed a napkin to assist in dabbing residue of tea from her mistress' gown. Dora quickly assembled all requisites for afternoon tea to the silver tray, and said, "Shall I bring fresh tea for two, ma'am?"

The duke looking on with top hat in hand denoted his visit as intentionally brief, though amusement danced in his eyes as he addressed Dora directly. "Tea for your mistress will do."

Estelle gained her feet, her pink gown ruined. "That will be all, Dora, and no tea at all."

The very second the door closed behind Dora, the duke again spoke. "Far be it from me to question why you are here alone and Rupert is lying prostrate at his house in the *crescent*, in what can only be described as repulsive opium induced haze. He is I might add unlikely to return here this evening."

Her heart dived, for news of Rupert's whereabouts and mention of opium confirmed her suspicions he still fell foul to the ghastly habit. "Did you come here just to discredit him and cause disharmony?"

"I came to ask if you are indeed married to my son, for it has come to my notice on trustworthy authority that Rupert referred to you as his future wife this very day. Now, is that the truth and you both lied to me; or did my informant mishear? Perhaps you would care to enlighten further."

She sensed a heated flush creeping up her throat and cloaking her face, and the duke was seeing it for himself. She could neither muster the will to deceive nor the words to defend the lie. He stepped close, his demeanour implying inner sense of rage, yet his hand to her cheek spoke of love.

"Estelle, Estelle," said he, almost a whisper. "You had all that I could give you in decent manner, and you had me body and soul if only you had known it, but it was never enough, was it?"

She must not respond. She must not lean into the palm of his hand. She must not let him stir the senses. She must not let his touch do wondrous things to her body. But a familiar frisson of pleasure rippled down her spine as his fingers drifted from cheek to neck, his hand thence cupping her head forcing her mouth close to his. "Please, don't do this to me."

"Kiss you and love you as I loved you before? It's been a year, Estelle, and my feelings for you are as fierce as ever. I am no fool and your silence reveals the truth. Marry my son and know that I shall be dying inside, a slow lingering death. The pain of this last year has been the forerunner to heartache I had never thought to encounter nor endure." He suddenly relinquished his hold upon her, stepped back a pace and bowed. "I shall not hold you to the bargain agreed upon within the library. Nonetheless Harper will paint a miniature of which you will deliver in person to Grosvenor House, that being my house in Bath." He reached into the pocket of his greatcoat. "Give me your hand."

Heart thumping she proffered her hand not expecting to be given a key. "What am I to do with this?" said she, the metal chilling to the touch and matching the coldness reflected in his voice.

"It is my sanctuary from the strife of marital and business affairs. The house overlooks Sydney Gardens. There is a brass plaque, which is easily spied by a coachman. Should I or my manservant be unavailable or absent from the premises when you call, the key speaks for itself. Deposit the miniature in my study of which lies on the second floor. Turn right at the top of the staircase and second door on the left. My manservant is of the utmost discretion, and be assured no questions will be asked of you should he answer to the bell-pull."

"That is all?"

Clearly impatient to take his leave a sigh escaped. "My dear Estelle, your delivery of the miniature ensures it will not fall into the wrong hands, nor displayed to others en route. I trust Harper to fulfil my commission, though in no way trust his honesty in keeping the image purely private between the three of us."

"I see, and this image will be to your personal taste?"

"Of course, I expect no less."

"Am I to trust Harper with his interpretation of your personal taste?"

"Trust me he will not dare misinterpret the instructions given."

"How can you be so sure of that? Portraitist's no doubt oft touch a client in assisting with the perfect pose and if I am as scantily clad as witnessed of Rose, it could be somewhat embarrassing."

The duke chuckled, his tone menacing in clarity. "Should he touch you improperly I shall cut off his hands."

"Presupposing I deign to tell you if inappropriate conduct occurs."

"There is always an element of the unknown in sitting for a portrait and who can say, you may well incite inappropriate conduct and thus enjoy it as you once enjoyed my indecent attentions upon you."

"You were but guilty of indecent inner desires, and I cannot say I ever felt threatened by the two occasions when you afforded exquisite pleasure the like I had never experienced before. You remained the epitome of a perfect gentleman whose self-restraint and abstention from indulging beyond touch and admiration of my body drove me mad with need and longing and you then left me in wanton and frustrated arousal."

A tentative smile twitched at the corner of his mouth. "Our affair was one of agreed mutual engagement and that of companionship in the first instance, of which I abided to. It was nine months into the companionable existence when I suggested a little innocent extra entertainment might prove fun, and yes, my attempts at pencil etchings and portraits were rudimentary at best. You were extremely tempting to the eye and I derived immense pleasure from asking you to leave off specific garments, of which became lesser in nature as our friendship grew stronger."

"We did have a good rapport, you and I, and it was not as easy to send that missive claiming I wished to end our arrangement as I had thought it would be. Yes, I had met Rupert, and attraction of sorts existed between us, and I think I made myself fall in love with him because I knew in my heart you could never fully commit in the way I had desired of you. Though even now, I am not sure what love truly is or how to recognise it for certain."

"You don't recognise love for what is?"

"How does one define the line between base lust and loving desire?"

He cast his top hat to her chair, unbuttoned his greatcoat, his expression clearly despairing the tragedy of her words. "My dearest Estelle," said he, catching up her hands. "Love is all encompassing. The heart thrums. Touch thrills. Tingles eddy down one's spine. Heady euphoria blinds to impediments and imperfections of those we fall in love with."

"I am not the least blind to Rupert's imperfections. I find it impossible to understand his need for opium. I despise it, and him for being so weak and under its spell. I thought I could live with it, cast it aside as though it is a harmless mistress that I must live with or lose him. I know that I will fight him and *it*, and we will inevitably fall to argument. Perhaps an irrevocable breach will then blight us in the same way you and the duchess live separate lives. I lived with a drunkard husband, and I can bear all that Rupert may fall foul to as long as I know I am loved."

"Estelle, Estelle," said he, drawing her close, his inner strength seeming as powerful as his physical presence. "All men have base needs, the difference in how they conduct themselves and the way in which they fulfil their desires is the mark of the inner man." He tilted her chin upward, forcing her eyes to level on his. "Tenderness and compassion to a woman's needs come easily to this man, where for others self-gratification remains uppermost and as often as not achieved in speedy manner. To say I am far from party to my son's levels of attendance upon a lady before taking his pleasure cannot be disputed, but perhaps his unmarried status is testament to his lacking finesse in matters of romancing and love. In that you have the advantage of knowledge gained from engagement, of which I envy him."

She dared not say Rupert engaged in tender manner with her, but when he did she always felt his heart belonged to someone else. Perhaps if truth be told Rupert's wealth had won her heart, not him. "You cannot expect me to reveal the intimate level of Rupert's indulgences, or mine for that matter."

"I have no need. Your eyes afford ample knowledge."

His lips embracing hers stilled her heart all but a second, the thrill pulsing down her spine thereafter as heady as his arm encircling her waist pressing her hard against him. How did he do that to her, ignite passion and intense desire, setting her alight with a burning need? She should disengage, cease the torment of his touch, cease the pleasure and be strong in resistance to any nuance of letting him see he had broken through her defences, defences she must again rebuild to protect her from the man she had once wished she could have.

Oh God, she must break free, must . . .

It was he who stopped kissing, and yet her arms were about his neck preventing his escape, his eyes revealing much she had not understood before or had refused to recognise. "Come to me, Estelle, and I swear, swear you shall be my wife in all but name. I cannot offer more than that."

"I think not. As your mistress I would be scorned by your friends and associates."

"It would not be like that for long. My friends and business acquaintances are not in the least ignorant to my situation at Huish Downham. Good God, you would not be the first mistress to take up residence in a duke's house, nor take on the role of a wife. Grosvenor House would be as good as yours, and believe it my darling girl my absences would be rare indeed barring brief visits to Huish Downham on matters of estate business. For I would not attend in the *Lords* and have you anywhere but in my London house awaiting my return."

"I cannot. I cannot abandon Rupert."

"Time will tell," said he, disengaging her arms from around his neck. "You have the key, and either I shall end up with a miniature portrait in my possession, or the lady herself will see fit to embrace my love, true love, and bestow the same mark of affection."

He snatched up his top hat and strode to the door and was gone.

Seven

Bath: October 18th

How was it possible to feel so relaxed?

Five days of sitting for her portrait could well have proved incredibly boring, but Harper was witty, quoted Shakespeare often, had a tendency to whistle whilst engrossed in his work, and would sometimes burst into song. He truly was a most likeable fellow, his black tussled hair constantly falling across his brow, which he tossed back or peered through as though quite shy, but his smile was that of a man of the world: all knowing, all seeing. As it was they had agreed to spread six sittings over three weeks for the large portrait, thus allowing half days for him to acquire new commissions and the other days to indulge his love of painting miniatures, which he claimed were far more time consuming than larger works.

As yet she had not spied one salacious miniature left lying around nor had he made mention of the miniature agreed upon beforehand. Two beautiful portraits of young children had caught her eye and she told him he had every reason to be proud of his fine work, for they were indeed a labour of love denoting his skill for mirror imaging.

Having sat that morning for nigh on two hours she mused how his studio although vast was extremely cluttered with an array of differing chairs, a settee, a small table and pencil sketches and discarded finished portraits and landscapes leaning against walls. It seemed he worked best with muddle all around him, and it afforded him the excuse to pretend he couldn't find things and thereby created sense of a hard-worked artist.

She liked him, liked his dedication to his craft and liked the way when he felt he had his pose perfect on canvas he would say, *'you may if you wish, relax your shoulders, move your hands and twiddle your toes'* the session having reached his exacting standards. She had learned much of portraiture and a little of the man standing behind his easel, for he had gladly explained how he always left faces as merely silhouettes until the very last for large portraits. He claimed by then he had the face mapped in his memory so that he could recall it when putting the final touches to the eyes. Whereas, with miniatures it was imperative to sketch a perfect face as quickly as able, especially when children were sitting for him, and the first thing he worked on tended to be the eyes.

His sudden movement of twirling his brush between fingers and placing it bristles upward in a pot and his striding across to the fireplace, displayed his usual unwillingness to let his client freeze to death in his attic, though it seemed more a case of need to warm his hands on this occasion. "It is as good as complete, and sooner than anticipated. Shall I press on? The light is good, but I'll quite understand if you would rather take your leave."

She fancied his breaking off at precisely noon was more to do with his need to visit the local tavern and partake of sustenance than letting her escape him. "If you are happy to let me go, then yes, I would appreciate having the early afternoon at my disposal."

He straightened up, rubbed his hands together, strode back to his brush and in one swift movement twirled it between his fingers and deposited it bristle down to another pot in which he left brushes soaking in foul smelling liquid. "That's me done, and I shall leave you in private." Equally deft of hand he hauled a hessian cloth up and over his easel to shroud the portrait from view. "No peeping or the magic of the completed portrait will be lost. Oh, and pop the key on the hook."

That was his cue for departure, and in haste he would pass word to her coachman at the nearby inn of her readiness to take her leave, thus allowing her the privacy to don a pelisse, bonnet and gloves and let herself out for he had no servants and wanted none. He had a woman who cleaned for him, washed his clothes and he ate at the inn. A strange existence but admirably suited to his chosen way of life, and no more outlandish than his trusting his client of today to lock the attic on departure and place the key on a hook inside the main door as had been the case since her second sitting. And likewise she would lock the outer door and place its key to a specific crack in the stonework.

Hardly before he was out of the door his footfalls heard on the bare board stairs, he was back and popped his head round the door a big grin. "You have a visitor, in the parlour."

With that said he was gone, and she supposed it to be Beatrice for the sweet thing had called by once before to see how the portrait was progressing and brought Harper a basket laden with fare. Harper on the other hand was of mind Beatrice came to spy on him for fear he was stealing her husband's livelihood, though he had made light of the notion.

Having met Beatrice and her sister Rose at afternoon tea taken with Georgette Lady Brockenbury, she had liked both sisters very much. Beatrice seemed too sweet to be overly concerned Harper's flare for attracting ladies to his cause would be detrimental to Ranulph, and on one occasion of Ranulph stopping by the studio he had expressed how glad he was Harper would lighten his workload. If anything Beatrice was worrying over Ranulph's desire to make arrangements for taking the family on a grand tour of Italy, whilst Rose was positively enthusiastic and saying how her sister must go and if they were blessed with a girl they could name her Florence or Venetia.

It was unfair to loiter in the attic whilst Beatrice waited below in the parlour where the fire would have long since become mere embers, and to alleviate the waiting time she hurriedly donned her pelisse, snatched up her bonnet and gloves and hastened from the attic. With the door locked it took but a moment to descend the upper stairs and enter the parlour: the visitor not as expected.

"*Rupert*?" exclaimed she, quite believing he was still in London on business, "what a lovely surprise."

"Is it?"

Why did he sound so brittle in response?

"Of course, but you gave me to understand you were to return on Monday next."

"Well, as you see, I am here now, though will not now return to Hazel Grove until the afternoon of Monday."

"Oh, I see."

"Mother's birthday falls on the Thursday, and I have strict instructions to attend for her dinner party and a day's hunting beforehand. A ball will be held on Friday, Saturday is set aside for a shoot, church and luncheon on Sunday, and come Monday I doubt I shall rise before noon."

"We have tonight."

"I cannot oblige, Estelle. That is why I am here in case you should hear of my return this day and think it odd indeed, for it occurred to me that if you were to pay visit to Georgette she would no doubt let slip the news of my return."

She always knew the day would come when he would have to attend at Huish Downham to her exclusion. "It was to be expected, and I bear no grudge at your attendance upon your mother."

"Then I can attend with a clear conscience."

She sensed air of detachment. That he was not telling all. That he had something on his mind and that he was seeking to avoid her company. She had every right to know why. "Indeed, but why can we not have this evening together? We've barely seen one another."

"That's the way of life. As it is, I received a message from a friend recently returned from India who is sadly in need of help, and I feel duty bound to offer assistance. So please bear with me on my absence for the next few days."

Where once she would have leaned forward and kissed him in show of affection, she held back. His stance was formal, rigid, unforgiving as though their harsh words on the eve of their return from Huish Downham still rankled and that he wished to end their relationship whilst lacking the courage to do so. He really was a man who had no desire to hurt women, they for the most part having hurt him in the past.

"Then I shall expect you on Monday."

"Monday," said he, a tentative smile, gesturing to the door. "Can I walk you to the inn and see you on your way?"

"I would like that."

As they left the cold parlour the chill of it followed and settled on her heart. What had seemed a bright future on leaving London and embracing the delights of Hazel Grove, now seemed as though she might end up back where she had come from. Something was wrong. Rupert had changed, or perhaps she had become too sensitive.

Eight

Huish Downham

Scent of fox lingered on the ether.

The hounds were baying on the far side of the woodland and for some strange reason his father had seemed less than enthusiastic for the greater part of the morning's hunt, though had indeed taken the lead in the last half hour or so and now ridden out of sight.

Trapped on a narrow path and slower riders up front, Rantchester spied his mother several riders distant. Impatient as ever her voice sharp she insisted less gossip might aid the idle riders on their way, and he was far from surprised when she suddenly reined her horse out of the line and began weaving her magnificent brute of a hunter through the trees to her left. The crashing of undergrowth and a path ready-made caused several riders to follow her initiative.

He followed too, for she was heading for a private ride where they could all urge their horses to the canter and make up for lost ground, for the hounds could be heard streaking away into the distance their quarry most certainly in sight.

Soon the cover of trees fell away and a short expanse of open heath stretched horses and *ri*ders at the gallop, his mother in grand fashion skirts billowing, ever urging her steed at a reckless pace toward a wall she had every intention of taking at the jump. She reined back a little and dropped to the canter, but unwilling to bide her time whilst a gentleman opened a gate to allow access to a bridleway, her son could only watch mesmerised as her horse rose from the ground and soared over the wall.

It happened so fast he couldn't be sure if her horse had clipped the wall or stumbled on impact with the ground. Heart in mouth he was already reining back as were other riders, men leaping from their mounts, the women crowding their horses close to the wall. His mother's horse did indeed lost its footing according to those closest to her.

The poor creature having rolled over seemed stunned, all the while horses milling beside the wall impeded Ranchester's efforts to leap over and tend to his mother. Upon finally reaching her twisted body he knew without a doubt her death was instantaneous, and it was many years since he had shed a tear in his mother's presence. There was nothing could be done for her except to cover her face with his coat, which he did and then turned to the distressed horse, now thrashing about in wild unrest. It finally regained its feet in shaky manner, its welfare his greatest concern.

Clearly tenderfoot on the off-front fore and barely able to place its hoof to the ground, as yet there was no heat to leg and no sure way of telling where the injury was situated. A rein had severed and the saddle lying part crushed on the ground suggested the horse had rolled over trapping his mother beneath, but given her position and that of the horse such was most unlikely.

Aware of a hand to his shoulder and something said, and others engaged in quiet discourse it became impossible to concentrate his mind, to think what he should do next. Thankfully someone had taken the initiative to send word ahead to his father, the sound of a horse departing at the canter setting precedence for those gathered around to thin out and take their leave; many sympathies in passing were expressed in kindly manner.

Soon there were but two men keeping company with him, Edwin Lord Brockenbury standing close to the late duchess as though guarding her lifeless body, and Frederick Davenport attending to their horses.

"I've sent for a wagon," said Edwin, dropping to his haunches, eyes on the partially crushed saddle.

"Thank you. I confess my mind fell utterly blank."

"Quite understandable, dear fellow, but you'd best take a look at the girth. I think we may need to call for the Constable."

"Whatever for? It was an accident, no doubt about that."

"Perhaps not, entirely," said Edwin. "Yes the horse stumbled, and yes the saddle came adrift, but if I am not mistaken this leather has a cut exactly where it is tore apart."

Frederick, an old comrade and fellow officer, leaned over the wall bettering his position to see the cut indicated by Edwin. "It does look suspect though a shoe nail could just as likely have scored the leather when the horse went down."

"How?" challenged Edwin.

"The horse rolled, and his leg trapped under his belly could well have torn the girth. It looks as though he may have torn a shoulder muscle into the bargain whilst thrashing about in getting his legs."

Edwin's lawyer brain had taken command in the first instance of his arriving on the scene, and now his mind as always thus ever sharp questioning the things around him as though they held answers to a riddle he had yet to solve. "Which side did it roll onto?"

"It matters not," replied Frederick, easing back from the wall, "the sheer impact against a sharp flint stone or piece of wood could have caused the girth to split."

"Perhaps your right," conceded Edwin.

Whilst regarding the saddle with less interest, Edwin nonetheless began eyeing the ground around it. Silence descended and the wait for the wagon seemed endless. Freddie had set to with concentrating his efforts in keeping three horses content with offerings of handfuls of plucked grass, while Edwin continued puzzling the tragedy from differing positions. Not that Rantchester minded all that much for his thoughts had drifted back in time to when his mother had for the first time bestowed nuance of affection toward him.

It was his seventh birthday as he recalled and his ravishingly beautiful mother had swept into the library clad in glorious red velvet riding attire, and had quite stolen his breath. In haste she had led him to the main entrance, and there presented him with a fine horse, and in the belief he had not ridden before she set to with teaching him the rudiments of horsemanship. Upon discovering he needed no tuition and that he was already proficient in saddle she had leaned across and hugged him, and said, *'Well little man, you make for a fine son'*.

The sudden sound of hooves thundering along the bridleway drew him from reverie, for the duke minus hounds had come alone without his usual entourage. As he reined back his horse from the canter to trot, his expression was that of much concern. "Well m' boy," said he, leaping from the saddle as able as any man of younger years. "Is she badly hurt?" Faced with a heavy silence, the awful truth dawned as he strode forward to see his wife shrouded beneath her son's coat. "Dear *God*. How; how did it happen?"

"Damn stupid question, father. The horse went down, mother is dead. How it happened matters not a jot."

"You are right, m' boy," returned his father, expression of deep sadness, "and what matters is getting her home in a dignified manner."

"*Dignified*? What's dignified about a woman cast to a wagon?"

"She'll ride home in a chaise. Nothing less." The duke immediately dropped to one knee beside his wife's body, and drew back Rupert's coat to reveal her face. "Damn it to hell, Constance," said he, his gloved hand brushing her cheek, "today of all days, and as reckless as ever in the thrill of the chase, no doubt about that."

It was the first act of affection bestowed upon his mother by his father and witnessed by self, and here she was dead on her fifty-third birthday. Watching his father with head lowered and sense of grieving appeared genuine enough, and yet this man of renowned attraction to ladies of all ages was now set free from a marriage that had given him nothing beyond that of heir to his title and a grand estate.

The duke regained his feet. "Go home, Rupert, and arrange for a carriage to collect your mother. I've already cancelled the hunt for today. After all, two foxes bagged made for good sport. Guests who are staying over will no doubt be waiting for news, and wondering whether they should take their leave or stay. I would prefer they leave of their own volition, but you know how it is sometimes, there are always those who outstay their welcome. I shall remain here until the carriage arrives."

"Edwin has already sent for a wagon."

"No matter, I want a carriage brought here directly."

"Go with Freddie, Rupert," said Edwin, stepping toward the injured horse, "and I shall keep company with his grace."

83

Whilst handing his mother's horse to Edwin's care their eyes met and he sensed his lawyer friend would probably mention the severed girth to the duke. "Don't say anything."

Edwin's response was much as expected. "Not for now. We can take a better look at the saddle, later. Oh, and take my horse with you. Your father or I will ride in the chaise."

Whilst clambering back over the wall his thoughts fell to Caroline, Lady Somerville, now back in town and staying over at the house. There was no denying she was hell-bent on regaining his heart. His every attempt to remain immune to her charms had already tested him in more ways than one since Estelle's coldness. Worse, his mother for the past two days had positively encouraged his keeping company with Caroline.

Needing time alone to think, to reason why Caroline could still lure his eye he had managed to evade her during the hunt by reining back and letting her take the lead, and had thence purposefully lost contact with her in the woodland. An able horsewoman she would have kept pace with the hounds and as everyone else, now on her way back to the house.

Reaching for the reins held in Freddie's care, it suddenly dawned on him how well his favoured chestnut had stood four-square in goodly manner alongside two companionable dark bays, when in normal circumstance the spritely animal resisted standing still for more than a moment or two. "It seems Huntsman has matured somewhat this day."

Whilst they both mounted their respective horses, Freddie said, "A few good gallops and with my old faithful Matlock here to keep him in check, it's fair to say young Huntsman has learned the bare bones of equine manners, true enough."

They set off, Freddie happy enough in leading Edwin's mount, the pair matching stride for stride at the trot and thence to the canter. Soon they were on approach to the woodland and again slowed to the trot. "So, Caroline Lady Somerville's husband disappeared somewhere in rebel territory," said Freddie, "and not a hair of his head having come to light."

"Better that he vanished, would you not say?"

"Had the rebels sent his horse back to the lines with its master's head in a bag and lashed to the saddle, as happened with other officers captured by rebels, there's no telling how it might have affected her. So yes, better she knows nothing of the ordeal he may have suffered before death embraced him. No children from the marriage, I take it?"

"Apparently not, nor did she seek to stay and marry a fellow officer who offered for her hand. She promptly booked passage for home shores and came directly to my mother seeking support in her grief, and mother welcomed her in the manner of a long lost child returned home at last. Damn it all, Caroline has family in the north and could have kept her distance and left me in peace."

"My lady wife is adamant the merry widow has it in mind to be a marchioness."

Ducking beneath trailing ivy cascading from the bough of an Ash tree, Rantchester indeed thought Rose was probably right. "And there lies the rub, for I have indeed helped Caroline in a momentary way until probate on Somerville's small estate is concluded."

"And?" queried Freddie, a widening grin. "Lordy be, you haven't—?"

"I haven't, though I cannot deny the lady remains a threat to my sanity."

"Ah . . . And what of the lovely Estelle?"

"Precisely."

"I do not envy your telling Estelle of Caroline's existence, and I'll wager you've made no mention of Estelle to Caroline."

"For the moment no, and I feel torn Freddie, torn by love for one and by sense of duty to the other."

"In my experience honesty is for the foolhardiest of the brave, and I'm a coward where women are concerned. While Rose remains blissfully ignorant to a moment of weakness in my past it cannot hurt her, and should she ever discover my shame it will surely hurt us both."

"How do I tell her, as I must?"

"Which one, dear fellow?"

He couldn't say, because he was unsure, unsure of his feelings at present. Estelle had his heart. Caroline never would, but there was unfinished business between them.

Nine

Monkton Heights.

Was it that time already?

Just as Georgette Lady Brockenbury's butler entered the drawing room; the chimes of the cased-clock in the hall declared four of afternoon. Conversation ceased momentarily, and Estelle could not help but study Rose Davenport. The charming lady herself handed her teacup and saucer directly to the butler as though he was indeed within their closed circle.

Rose was a striking woman with high cheek bones. Her blue eyes were sharp and there was a defined sense of inquisitiveness about her, and her copper coloured hair beautifully enhanced by deep blue silk gown; there was no doubting Rose was Beatrice Brockenbury's sister, and equally as likeable.

The butler's presence proved no deterrent to Rose, who clearly had something amusing to import, for she laughed softly, and said, "Can you imagine what Freddie said when he heard Caroline Lady Somerville had returned to England, and thence to Bath of all places. He was truly astounded and declared it a provocative gesture."

"As I understand it, Caroline is staying at Huish Downham," said her ladyship.

With deftness of hand the tea things were gathered and placed to a silver tray and the butler retreated, as though unseen and unheard by Rose or her ladyship.

"Oh . . . then she will be out hunting today . . . Good *Lord*, poor Rupert," said Rose.

"Indeed," returned her ladyship, shifting a little on her favoured chaise longue as though a tad uncomfortable. "We must not give sway to speculation, for Rupert's circumstances have changed markedly, and Estelle has yet to make Caroline's acquaintance."

Rose blushed. "Oh lordy, Estelle, I should not have mentioned the damn woman."

It was unfair to expect her newfound friends to refrain from discussing people of whom she was unacquainted, and to garner knowledge was a markedly sensible thing to do. "I know not what she did, presumably to Rupert, for he has never mentioned her. I am not sure I wish to know, but feel if enlightened, I will be prepared for any eventuality that might arise from this lady's return and presence at Huish Downham."

Georgette Lady Brockenbury again shifted her position. "Estelle, it is not for us to enlighten you, beyond the fact Caroline once meant a great deal to Rupert."

"*Please*, I regard you as a trusted friend, and would much appreciate a level of insight as to what occurred between Rupert and this Caroline you speak of."

"It was all of four years past when Caroline married Somerville and sailed with him to India. No one knows for sure why she chose Hubert Somerville over Rupert, when it was thought they were madly in love. Though Edwin and I always had our doubts Rupert was ever that sincere. It was mooted the fault lay with Rupert, that had he asked her to marry him she would have said yes, but he didn't and Hubert did."

"When the news broke of her marriage by special licence," said Rose, laying a hand to Estelle's in compassionate manner, "It was said Rupert was devastated but no one had thought he would just disappear."

"He loved her that much?"

Rose grimaced. "I never thought he did, nor did Freddie."

"She was Rupert's mistress," said her ladyship, "and affection of sorts undoubtedly existed between them."

Rose looked unconvinced. "Freddie has always claimed Caroline led Rupert to the dark side of opium."

"We cannot be sure that is so," intoned her ladyship, "though her outlandish behaviour was quite shocking at times."

"Oh dear, I do so love gossip and gossiping with close friends, and telling tales on Caroline is infinitely satisfying. I have not forgotten her little antic with Freddie, and my darling husband was so*ooooo* embarrassed by it all." Rose laughed. "Do you remember the incident Georgette, the day I pushed her in the fountain at Lady Bathurst's summer ball?"

"I do, and I think I may have done the very same had she straddled my husband's back in the manner of riding astride a horse, and giggling loudly enough to draw attention to his embarrassment."

She had to know and asked, "And Rupert was with her?"

Rose chuckled, her triumph over Caroline memorable. "It is a tad remiss of me to assume, dear Estelle, you should think of me as a loving friend upon a mere second encounter. But I feel the three of us, not to mention my dear sister B, have a duty to bond for the sake of our men folk who are friends of longstanding." She laughed, and furthered with, "Caroline is a whore born and bred, and as near the dark side of life as you will ever meet in your lifetime, Estelle, and really not worthy of mention."

Although Rose was prone to gossip, as Beatrice had long since informed her, it was said Rose only gossiped within the confines of their extended family. "Please, Rose.

Tell me what you know of Rupert's disappearance."

"Well now. His father sent out search parties fearing the worst, not knowing if he was indeed alive. Rumours were circulating to the effect he had indeed gone after Caroline, though no one could find evidence of his having taken passage for India. His father became quite distraught until my brother-in-law, Ranulph, thought he might be found closer to home than first imagined. Indeed he was, and to the duke's dismay, Rupert was in a *sorry* state of mind."

She hated to say it but knew in her heart where they had found him. "An opium den . . . I presume?"

"Afraid so," replied Rose.

"The past is the past," intoned her ladyship, "and Rupert has Estelle, now."

"I am not sure that he does, or I, him."

Astonishment swept to both the lovely faces before her, and neither it seemed were able to muster words to express their thoughts.

"I have a past, too, and some might say a dark past."

"Oh do tell, Estelle," said Rose, a warm smile. "Think of us as your sister. What is said between us will stay with us, and B, of course."

She could not help but laugh, and it lightened the mood, for her ladyship let slip a smile declaring Rose had spoken the truth. "We are curious, that is all, and unlike Rose, I too have several bones in my closet," declared her ladyship.

"I see no point in denying I had two gentlemen friends before I met Rupert, and to my chagrin, the very same officer who caused a scene outside White's Coffee House."

"Oh lordy," exclaimed Rose. "Not Finch?"

"Indeed, though it was but a short-lived acquaintance."

"I confess I never liked the man." Rose turned to Georgette. "Do you remember Captain Finch? He was present at the Summer Ball the night." Rose clapped her hand to mouth. "I am so sorry, Georgette, for we promised never to broach that night, ever again."

Her ladyship shrugged. "It matters not, for it was a long time ago."

"Yes, but James perished that night at Monkton Abbeyfields. And beastly Adam, his brother of all people, shot him as it turned out."

"That is true, and Rupert and I later had a part to play in Adam's death. Unwittingly so, and if not for our foolhardy plan to uncover the truth of that dreadful night, Eliza would not have killed Adam, nor set fire to the house." Her ladyship waved both hands to prevent Rose from uttering another word. "*Please*, do continue, Estelle. You were saying—"

Had she heard right, murders as opposed to murder at the ruined house the other side of lake? Goodness, it seemed there was much she had yet to learn about the Brockenbury men, but casting thoughts to one side, she said, "It is rather difficult to explain why I have misgivings about my feelings for Rupert, but you see, there was a man I had become very fond of and he was still a part of my life when I met Rupert. At the time there seemed no hope of this other gentleman ever advancing our relationship to more than that of, well . . . that of friend."

Rose beamed a knowing smile. "Ha, so like a man. Was he married do you think?"

"I had it in mind he was, for he always withheld knowledge of his life beyond London, and Rupert was so sweet and attentive I truly wanted to fall in love with him. It naturally seemed only right and proper to dispatch a missive to my gentleman friend severing all contact, for I thought I had fallen for Rupert, and truly thought myself in love with him when I moved to Hazel Grove."

91

"And now," said her ladyship, "you fear your heart has lost its way a little, is that not so?"

"Oh goodness me," said Rose, a hearty and reassuring smile, "it's merely cold feet you are feeling, and come the day of your wedding your heart will positively burst with happiness."

"But you see I cannot deny a piece of my heart may dwell elsewhere."

"Oh lordy," said Rose.

"Would this be your earlier gentleman friend?" enquired her ladyship.

"It is, and I know not what to do, for I have encountered him again and have tried my very best to exclude him from my thoughts."

Rose tittered. "And he wishes to resume your former acquaintance, no doubt."

"Of course he does," said her ladyship, admonishing Rose for stating the obvious. "Dearest Estelle, no wonder you are torn, for you clearly have great affection for this man if a little hurt by his prior motives for secrecy. But are you any the wiser as to his secret existence?"

She could not deny Rose and Georgette were extending sisterly warmth and not the least bit judgemental in the face of her declaration. "Yes, I do have the facts and sad they are, and the life that he leads is strange, albeit a necessary one."

"Do we know him?" asked Rose, eyes wide in hope of gaining insight. "After all, a secret shared may lighten your burden a little."

"He has a substantial estate not far from Bath and a town house, and if I should choose to accommodate his wishes to renew our affections, the house in Bath is readily at my disposal."

Rose straightened up a little. "As his mistress?"

"That is all I can be in name, though in his heart I will be the wife he has never had."

"I suspect we are well acquainted with this man but shall not press for his name." Her ladyship's expression suggested Rupert was of prime concern to her. "I can only pray that if this man wins your heart that you are kindly in setting Rupert free from his obligation toward you, for Rose and I know all too well of his reaction to Caroline's hasty marriage to Somerville."

"It is because of Rupert that I pray for guidance in this matter, for of late he has seemed somewhat indifferent, distancing himself from my company and I know not why."

Her ladyship eased her feet from her favoured *chaise.* "Perhaps he senses your plight, not knowing if he has failed you in some matter of great importance to *you.* Men can be so blind to the obvious and tend toward distancing themselves rather than seeking to discover what ails a woman."

"I can testify to that," said Rose, "for Freddie quite thought I had a fancy for young Harper, my brother-in-law's student, apprentice, call him what you will. It was all a rather silly misunderstanding, and entirely due to secrecy for my part. And me being me, all innocence itself, I thought I could have a miniature portrait painted for Freddie's birthday, a special portrait for his eyes only and without his suspecting a thing of my frequent and unaccountable outings."

"Did you?" exclaimed Georgette. "Goodness."

Quite unabashed, Rose chuckled. "Oh it was nothing terribly risqué, though it did require my undressing beforehand. I wished the image to have a Romanesque ambience, thus I had a length of the finest silk draped across my person."

"A provocative pose?" enquired her ladyship, amusement dancing in her eyes.

"It was for Freddie's eyes only."

"And Harper's," said Georgette, a giggle, "and I do see Freddie's concern in that aspect of the sittings."

"Harper was kindness itself, and his flattery toward a lady is always quite harmless. As it is Ranulph was present throughout the sittings. They shared the studio back then, and Ranulph set Freddie straight and said how foolish he was in letting his imagination take hold, and that Beatrice had arranged the cloth whilst the men remained absent from the room."

"And the miniature," said Georgette, twiddling her toes, "did Freddie appreciate his birthday gift?"

"The day he stormed into the studio ranting and raving, the portrait was almost finished and after one fleeting glance at the miniature destined for the inside of a pocket watch, he snatched it from Harper and cast it through a window left open. Harper upped and ran for his life out into the garden, where he and Beatrice searched for the portrait but failed to find it."

Estelle dared not say Harper must have found the miniature. Nor dare she inform Rose the Duke of Leighdon had that very miniature within his possession. Nor could she say it was completed and a decidedly provocative piece of artwork it was, too.

There was a light tap at the door, which preceded the butler's appearance. "Ma'am," said he, addressing her ladyship. "His lordship has sent word from Huish Downham to the effect he cannot make it back in time for dinner this eventide, and will return here on the morrow as soon as able."

"Is that all?" snapped Georgette. "No reason for his delay?"

"No ma'am. I did however enquire of the young lad who galloped in did he know why his lordship had sent word of his delay. Apparently a tragic death occurred in the hunting field this morning."

"Did he say who had perished and how?"

"Not how ma'am, only that it is a family matter and the Constable arrived at Huish Downham whilst he was departing."

"Thank you, Taylor, and hold for a moment." Her ladyship cast her eye across the divide, and Estelle's heart stalled. "Do you wish to have your carriage brought to the door?"

Could fate have played a cruel trick on her? "Dear God, who can it be?"

Rose let forth a sigh, a sigh of relief. "Oh lordy, my heart leapt to mouth for fear it was Freddie. And Georgette is right. You must go straight away to Huish Downham, Estelle. Would you like it if I came too? I am most happy to oblige."

"Yes, yes, I would so appreciate your company, for it is unlikely I shall be allowed to enter the house." For a brief moment the room wavered before her eyes, Georgette's voice drifted on the ether, the butler's too and his swift departure barely noticed. "The duchess, you see, I am not allowed to meet with the duchess."

"Oh poppycock," said Rose, getting to her feet, "Constance is a fine woman, and the least likely of all the matriarchs hereabouts to miss the chance of acquaintance with a mistress or two. She thrives on gossip with the best of us, and as much as the duke has attempted to spare her the sordid details of Rupert's past, she has herself said often enough, he is no saint but he is her son."

"Take heart, Estelle," said Georgette. "Constance Duchess of Leighdon prefers the company of brave females borne of the *noblesse militaire,* and no doubt that is why she took pity on Lady Caroline. She despises heartless aristocratic loonies of her own ilk, and pours scorn on their weakness in bowing to tradition and thence suffering the indignity of loveless marriages, and all for the sake of advancing family fortunes. Such sweeping generalisation excludes my parents who were madly in love from day one to the day they were robbed of life in a tragic coaching accident."

"Indeed, it is fair to say the duchess regrets to this day her own weakness in marrying the duke, when her heart had long belonged to another," said Rose, casting a tentative smile. "So let us go in good heart, and pray Rupert is safe."

"But if the duchess favours Lady Caroline and wishes Rupert wedded to her, will she not view me as a needless obstacle?"

"I think not, for she will look upon both of you as sporting game and will be much amused to see who will win his favour." Rose sighed, as though a romantic game of chess would decide the fates of Estelle and Caroline. "As it is, you have the advantage, Estelle. You have Hazel Grove and Rupert is there most days, is he not? Caroline, the poor unfortunate, relies on the charitable nature of persons willing to provide free board and lodging. To his credit, Rupert has not obliged with affording Caroline the use of his house in The Royal Crescent."

"I wish I could say Rupert has shared in my company the past couple of weeks. But in all honesty, his Royal Crescent abode has seen more of him than I have."

A tap at the door once again preceded the butler, his arm shrouded with one green fur-trimmed wool pelisse, and a dark blue one. He said, "Ma'am, the Marquis of Rantchester's carriage is now at the door."

"Then we must away," said Rose, relieving Taylor of her blue pelisse. "The sooner the better and you can stop off here on the way back, can't you, Estelle? Though I suppose, I could just as easily alight at Fenemore Cottage." She turned to the butler. "Could you see my carriage is sent home?"

"Of course, right away, Mrs. Davenport."

Taylor assisted with seeing the green pelisse to her shoulders, whilst her ladyship hastily helped Rose to don her glorious blue one. "I would appreciate your dropping in with news on your way back," said her ladyship, "for my thoughts will be with you and I fear I shall not settle to sleep this night if left pondering Rupert's fate in what has occurred this day."

"Then we shall stop by," said Rose, "won't we, Estelle?"

"Yes, we will, and please don't fret too much."

"Away with both of you, and pray God for the mercy of the deceased."

Ten

Huish Downham

They were at their destination.

The journey from Monkton Heights had thankfully passed without incident despite the weather turning for the worst en route. Conditions were now treacherous on the ride leading down to the house from the main gates, which caused the carriage to slew on occasion of its wheels losing traction.

Where they had waved to Georgette standing on the front step beneath glorious sunshine, indeed for the first few miles the pleasant weather had served to keep their eyes keened to the countryside. The sight of brambles laden with blackberries and that of wild briars weighing heavy with scarlet rosehips had admirably distracted Rose. Talk of jam and jelly making and scones became her theme for a mile or two. In turn the delights to be gathered from hedgerows had diverted Estelle's thoughts from the awfulness that might be waiting ahead. But no more than four miles along the highway the sky had turned grey and their thoughts and words with it.

Now eight miles distant from Georgette, locked in silence their eyes to the rain lashing against the windows of the carriage and the relentless sound of it hammering on the canopy, the vehicle was finally rumbling past the front of Huish Downham and rolling under the *porte-cochère*. It came to a rather abrupt halt the carriage swaying.

All but a few moments having passed, Pettigrew, the duke's butler appeared on the step, his expression one of grief, whether feigned or genuine quite impossible to judge.

Rose, not one for overt formality opened the carriage door and alighted before Pettigrew could assist.

Clearly acquainted with the arrogant butler, she said, "Ah, Pettigrew, we were most concerned on hearing the news of the tragic accident, and felt we had to come directly. You see, we must know; is the marquis in good health?"

"Indeed Mrs. Davenport. The marquis is hale and hearty, though at present indisposed."

Estelle remained seated her heart still drumming despite the good news, fear gripping her as she sank farther into the shadows of the carriage. She could not, simply could not face Pettigrew. He indeed looked beyond Rose, his eyes seeking sight of the second half of the *we*. Perhaps reflection on the glass prevented his seeing her, and he made no move to intrude upon whomever, though no doubt he had it in mind exactly who was seated in the carriage.

"And my husband?" enquired Rose.

"I shall inform him you are here."

He gestured for Rose to step inside. She refused and stepped back to the carriage, just as they had planned whilst they were on approach to the main gates. "Could you ask him to attend upon me out here?"

Pettigrew's expression implied disbelief, his eyes once again set hard in the direction of the carriage. "If that is your wish."

"It is."

He retreated, leaving the main door pushed to frame but open.

Rose ascended into the carriage. "Are you sure this is a wise decision, Estelle? There are many guests staying here at the house, and should any one of them have spied Rupert's carriage on approach, it is likely questions will be asked as to why it is here. It may be construed he is leaving

100

for some reason, when in the circumstances of a death in the family such is most unlikely."

"We agreed we would establish who died and then take our leave."

"That is true, and we shall express our condolences. Pettigrew will deliver our heartfelt message word for word. He equals the best of talking parrots that I have had the misfortune to encounter."

Estelle almost laughed, drawing an amused response from Rose.

"There," said she, her tone motherly as though soothing an anguished child, "I swear I saw a speck of light in your eyes and hint of a smile."

The carriage jolted; the horses seemingly as restless as she and just as eager to take flight. "I do appreciate your forbearance in this, and goodness knows what your Freddie will think of my hiding here in the carriage."

"Believe me, Estelle, Freddie is very understanding of women. Me in particular. I do have the strangest of notions at times."

"Rose *Davenport*." The sing-song cry of a female voice startled both to the presence of purple hue on the doorstep. "Come out, come out, I know you are there."

"Oh lordy," whispered Rose, "it's Caroline."

This was worse case scenario, and Rose quick thinking leapt to her feet and almost tumbled on top of Caroline who hastened to the carriage in a blur of purple silk. "Goodness, I had not thought to see you here," fibbed Rose, a generous embrace bestowed to the other woman, "and sincere commiserations, dear heart, in your loss."

"Heavens Rose, I am most fortunate in my loss," said Caroline, the rustle of a sumptuous gown the deepest shade of purple accentuated by the way in which she gathered up her skirts in readiness to turn about. "Hubert has left me well provided for. There's a castle don't you know, though tiresomely north of the border and I cannot lay my hand on a penny of his damned estate for the present."

"Oh dear, then how shall you manage your affairs?"

Rose by good fortune of standing before the carriage door blocked view of skirts behind her, which in itself would tell Caroline of another presence. Nonetheless the raven-haired, dark-eyed widow reached for the open carriage door and glanced behind it, presumably to view the crest on the outer panel.

"Well, well," said she, looking Rose in the eye. "I rather thought this was Rupert's carriage. Are you now a dark horse lady?" She laughed, as though mocking the very suggestion she had in mind. "Have I missed on a vital piece of gossip, and you and Rupert are . . . how shall I say?"

"We are not, but you see," said Rose, linking her arm with Caroline's, "I came post-haste from Georgette Lady Brockenbury's, just to set all our minds at rest in knowing Rupert and the duke are safe and well." Leading Caroline toward the house door, she furthered with, "And the carriage just so happened to be at Monkton Heights. How is the duke in this time of great sadness?"

Caroline glanced over her shoulder, her expression implying element of confusion as though sure eyes were upon her. "Indeed the duke is bearing his loss as well as can be expected. Rupert on the other hand, poor love. Well . . . such a shocking way to lose his mother."

Estelle let forth a sigh of relief at the news the duke was safe from harm, her heart nonetheless extending to Rupert. So it was her grace who had met with a terrible accident. She should go to Rupert, tend to his hurting, soothe his pain, and even though she now knew the duchess was dead she could not bear to step across the threshold of Huish Downham. Unlike Caroline who seemed at home in the vastness of the palatial residence, to Estelle, the house posed a danger to her. It was a place where her heart could be torn asunder, Rupert's too if she held him to his pledge. She could not knowingly marry a man trapped by word of honour when his heart lay elsewhere, and indeed it seemed that way for since Caroline's return Rupert had become remote.

She blessed the shadowy interior of the carriage, for there were so many things in need of careful thought. A shiver rippled down her spine as she glanced toward the house door. The grief from within seemed as though drifting toward her; a deathly ether entering her small space and drawing her to its darkness. Her thoughts too slipped to the past and that of her life as merely the wife of a cavalry captain and the daughter of a cavalry colonel. She had known her place in society back then and no ambition to step beyond it. Then the death of Harry and her loving father, one quickly followed by the other had torn her world apart.

Losing the two men who had meant such a great deal to her had seemed so unfair at the time, her widowhood thence posing problematic for friends. After all, two at a table was companionable. Three at a table were mismatched. Four at a table were enough hands for a decent game of cards. Thus invitations to dinner became fewer and fewer when attempts at matchmaking by her hosts failed. Her resistance to entertain the notion of discreet courtship with fellow officers of her husband's regiment had duly fallen foul of the wives desperate to see her at least betrothed to another man as soon as could be arranged. She did relent on one occasion to appease her friends and in so doing broke her own promise to abide to a decent period of mourning, and her foolhardiness led to a disastrous affair with Finch.

There were times in the midst of her grief when she felt blessed her short marriage had left her childless and no little person to worry about. At other times she had longed for someone of her own to love, and a moment of madness had led her to the arms of Captain Finch. Then along came the duke posing as Malcolm Uffington, the kindly gentleman who turned her life around and gave her a taste of a life she had dreamed of and never believed possible. Then there was Rupert and her life now again in flux, her direction unknown.

Casting a glance beyond the *porte-cochère* to the parkland, the grey leaden sky matched her greyness of mind: the trees stark in their blackness as though devoid of colour too. The carriage suddenly swayed and Freddie Davenport leapt aboard, his fairness not so dissimilar to Rupert which for a moment caused her heart to dive.

"Rose whispered in my ear you were out here." Seating himself across from her, he furthered with, "Why in God's name are you hiding in the carriage?"

"I am loath to step inside the house, and please, I would prefer if Rupert knows nothing of my coming here."

"Far be it from me to attempt to fathom your reason, though I'll wager Catherine Lady Somerville has a part to play in your reluctance to show face."

"She seems charming and fittingly suited to Huish Downham."

"Ah," said Freddie, a big grin, "you see her as your rival."

"I know very little about her and cannot be so singularly minded in determining the lady as a rival or not."

Freddie chuckled. "I'll tell you this. She's a lady by title and no lady by nature. Caroline takes what Caroline wants."

"Are you saying she wants Rupert?"

"I am of mind she will endeavour to regain his trust and Rupert is exceedingly disturbed by the way in which the duchess met her death. By the by, her grace was a fine horsewoman and her saddle is under close scrutiny as we speak."

"Why for?"

"Lord Brockenbury is convinced the girth was slashed prior to the accident."

"And what is your opinion?"

"Sceptical at first glance, but Edwin has put forth a convincing argument. The leather at close quarter does indeed look as though a blade may have purposefully weakened the strength of the girth when at full-stretch."

"Does . . . Did the duchess have enemies who would wish harm upon her?"

"None, according to the duke, and Rupert's half sisters cannot recall any incident between the duchess and that of dismissed staff which might have led to a grievance of any worth."

"Then perhaps it was indeed a misfortunate accident."

Freddie shrugged. "Who can say, and we may never unravel the mystery. It's not as though the duke has a mistress hidden away and of mind to make her his duchess, albeit he dismisses Edwin's theory as ludicrous." Freddie's sudden laughter strafed the air. "On the other hand, should his grace perish in strange circumstances in the near future, I shall place my wager on sweet Caroline as the murderess."

"Oh I see, and her then marching Rupert to the marital bedchamber and becoming the new duchess instead of mere marchioness."

"That's about the measure of my thoughts on intrigues of the heart and the dark and dangerous Caroline."

"She is decidedly attractive."

"There is a species of lusty male spider who think precisely that of females prior to mating, and duly suffer the consequences of being eaten alive by the very one they desired in the heat of the moment."

If only he knew it the woman sitting before him was getting the measure of Freddie, and it seemed likely he had indeed fallen victim to a tempting female and paid the price for momentary rash indulgence. It would be unfair to ask him how much he might have paid for a woman's silence, for he was a good and loving husband to Rose and doting father to their children. He had undoubtedly learned a lesson and very unlikely to repeat the same mistake again.

As silence hung on the air between them, Rose came rushing forth from the house. "We must leave, right away if you wish to remain incognito, Estelle. And Freddie, dearest, Rupert is looking for you. I escaped unseen by him, but Caroline will surely tell him I am here and rode here in his carriage."

Freddie fair flew from the carriage, kissed his wife most passionate, helped her aboard and closed the carriage door. He then shouted to the coachman. "Monkton Heights, my good man, and smart about it."

As he then fled into the house, they in turn took flight from Huish Downham.

Eleven

She would be home, soon enough, and all but a mile distant from Fenemore Cottage, Estelle envied Rose who was already safe at home beside a cosy fire. It was now quite chill in the carriage and with three miles of rain-lashed highway still before her she pondered the fast fading light. Travelling without a companion was a lonely experience, and all manner of dark thoughts involving tales of rogues on the highways crept to mind. Whilst living in London she had only ever ventured onto the streets after sunset in company with a gentleman, and usually by carriage.

And yet, upon her arrival in the district of Bath it was pleasing to learn that vagabonds in and around the city had become as rare as sightings of highwaymen in the countryside. But in recent weeks several mail coaches had been forced to a standstill and the occupants robbed. In one such case the armed guard atop the mail coach was killed, and the felon was still at large. The Constable claimed the man had local knowledge, thus meaning a man within one of the village communities surrounding Bath had taken to the evil side of life. Local villagers' were thence worried one of their own had betrayed their trust, but who could it be?

It was oft implied the local militia and the district Constable were indeed a formidable force. It was further voiced *'that whomever had shot the mail guard, the felon had best be quaking in his boots, for the Constable would never let him rest easy until his body ceased swinging from the gallows'*. She shuddered at the very thought of the gallows, a device Edwin Lord Brockenbury no doubt pondered often when sitting in judgment on cases of murder or that of other heinous crimes.

She sensed the carriage beginning to slow in readiness to take a turn from the highway to the byway. The light outside was still sufficient to map her course, and the familiar landmark of a whitewashed cottage suddenly materialised and vanished from view. A spinney came next where tree trunks, boughs and branches intertwined creating strange shapes. It was all too easy to visualise humans lurking within and peering from behind trees. Worse, as the carriage began its swing to the right, branches brushed against the windows as though clawing to get inside. Even when the cover of trees fell away the leaves left clinging to the glass fought to stay aloft against the rain swilling ever downward.

Hazel Grove beckoned at three miles distant and her heart went out to the coachman and groom sitting aloft: the conditions appalling. They were good honest fellows and much treasured by Rupert. Although he rarely praised them in public, out of their hearing he acclaimed them as superb in handling his team of horses. She had a notion they knew their master appreciated all they did for him, especially young Jem. Yes, she would be sorry to see them go, for they had indeed served her equally well. Nevertheless, her mind was made up. After a good night of rest they would on the morrow depart from Hazel Grove and take with them a letter for Rupert.

The governess cart in the barn belonged to the house, and would adequately serve purpose for getting out and about. After all, if members of her household staff could drive it to and from Bath so could she. It might take a few turns around the paddocks and along the driveway in order to familiarise herself in how to drive a horse, but surely such was not so difficult to accomplish. She could then pay

108

visit to the saddler and arrange to purchase a side saddle, and perhaps acquire a horse quite soon. Where from she knew not, surmising the saddler would know to whom she could turn to for a suitable mount. At least she was proficient in saddle and quite able at handling a fractious horse, something Rupert had applauded whilst taking a ride in Hyde Park when her hired mount pestered by a horse fly had become exceedingly skittish.

Happy days back then.

She had other worries now and a word with Georgette Lady Brockenbury had to be of prime importance, for there was no feasible means of affording the rent for Hazel Grove. She really would be sorry to leave Georgette's beautiful country house. A modest abode was all she could stretch to in order to retain at least some of her household staff.

Deep sense of loneliness suddenly befell her and she had not wanted to cry, had not wanted to accept she was living a lie. How sad it all was the way life could take such a cruel turn and leave one feeling bereft all over again. The day's tragedy had touched her and tainted her, for her heart had known where it was leading her and now she could not follow it. She could never step across the social boundary and embrace her heart's desire, for to do so could well prove fatal for the man who had truly won her heart. He had his family now, and friends would surely rally to his side in the bleak days ahead. It grieved nonetheless to think she could not help Rupert, and she was not even sure a letter would help in easing his pain.

Wiping away a tear from her cheek, she could only pray a suitable house could be found and a goodly distance from Bath. Perhaps it might be worth venturing south, maybe even as far as Devon where Harry's family dwelled. She had not set eyes upon his brothers and sisters in so long she

109

could barely visualise any one of them, though letters were still readily exchanged at Christmas tide.

A deep sigh escaped: the loneliness gripping her.

No longer cognisant to distance travelled and little light to see by; the carriage slowing to a halt was not so unusual. The carriage lamps would need lighting and the task was nigh impossible whilst moving along at a walking pace let alone at the trot. Jem's voice soon drifted on the restless wind, the coachman responding. The rain thankfully ceased hammering on the canopy, and the carriage door was suddenly wrenched wide to reveal a rain-soaked man wearing a greatcoat, a muffler part shielding his face and hat tipped forward, presumably to protect from the prior torrential downpour. If not for his mellow voice she would have shrunk to the corner in fear for her life.

"Your Grace," said she, as he clambered aboard and settled across from her.

She dared say no more as Jem retreated into the darkness leading a horse to the rear of the carriage. All but a few minutes the groom returned and closed the door on passing to the fore, and the duke's insane halting of the coach must have caused a moment of fear for Jem and the coachman.

Embarrassed by the duke's audacity and his insanity of setting out on horseback in foul weather, she challenged him outright her ferocity apparent. "Are you *mad*? A man attired in black, a muffler to face and astride a horse . . . Dear God, Jem might have shot you."

"Mad indeed," replied the duke, a mere whisper whilst casting his hat beside him on the seat. "I am utterly soaked to the skin, and indeed, thanks to the *Almighty*, Jem recognised my horse."

She fell to whispering too. "Why stop the carriage? Why did you not ride directly to Hazel Grove and wait there until

110

my return? Though I cannot imagine why you have paid visit."

The carriage gave a jolt and again trundled on its way, the wind and wheels on stone enough to drown their voices and no need for whispered discourse.

"I went directly to Hazel Grove and waited there until I could bear it no longer. Might I ask why you've been away so long? Damn it all, Estelle, I spied the carriage departing from Huish Downham and as soon as etiquette permitted I took leave of my guests on the pretence of business in Bath, and promptly set out after you."

"I promised Georgette we would call back at Monkton to set her mind at rest, for she feared Rupert might have met with an accident. Then we travelled the short distance to Fenemore Cottage and here I am, quite cold and wanting nothing more than something warm to drink, something to eat, and a fire in the hearth."

"Why did you remain in the carriage whilst at Huish?"

"It seemed right and proper, for I could hardly intrude upon your grief and the family's grief at such a time."

"You are supposedly my son's wife, or have you forgotten the lie told to my butler? Is it any wonder Pettigrew came to me expressing concern to the effect he thought it likely you were sitting outside in the carriage, though claimed he could not rightly be sure it was the marchioness who had accompanied Rose Davenport to the house. To say Pettigrew was confused is to understate what he was surmising. I know the man too well."

"He saw me not, and to all intents and purposes Rose was the only person conveyed there by the carriage."

"Accursed weather," said his grace, peeling a sodden leather glove from his hand. "I concede it may have looked that way to the less observant. Pettigrew on the other hand is noted for seeing what cannot be seen."

111

"A nose as good as your hounds, it would seem."

As he peeled away the second glove and placed both with his hat, he said, "Time is short, Estelle, and dancing around the why and wherefore of your sitting in this carriage whilst Caroline Lady Somerville is paying court to Rupert, is pointless indeed." A chuckle suddenly strafed the air as though mocking his own madness for riding through a storm in pursuit of a runaway. "If you think I am here to flatter you and beg you to reconsider my affections toward you, then you are sorely mistaken. I felt I had your answer when I gave you the key to Grosvenor House, your eyes said much, and I am here for no other purpose than that of establishing whether you love my son or not. If you do, then your presence at Huish Downham is called for. If on the other hand you are having second doubts about Rupert, there is little I can do that will help in solving your dilemma."

Her worst nightmare was sitting across from her, his words denouncing any sense of affection they had once shared. But she had no right to expect otherwise from his grace. "I always suspected Rupert's heart could never be truly mine, and that someone forever plagued his thoughts. I have oft pondered why does he turn to opium if I am all that he wants?"

"Estelle," said his grace, leaning forward with elbows to knees, "fight for him, if you want him. Let him see that he made the right choice with you, for if he turns to Caroline she may well destroy him."

"But don't you see. I don't think I ever *had* him." How many times must she say this to differing people for them to understand she foresaw marriage with Rupert deteriorating to that as endured by his father and mother: unloved and lonely and each in their own hell. "I have no desire to fight for a man of whom I know to be secretly in love with

112

another woman. He toyed with my life and I foolishly let him, and I now wish to start anew and become myself again. I shall not have the wherewithal to remain at Hazel Grove and will instead seek modest accommodation more suited to my social standing."

"Dear God, Estelle," said he, reaching for her hands, his touch gentle in clasping both. "My dearest girl, you cannot simply walk away."

She wished he had not crossed the divide, his touch unbearable, her heart beating too fast, and his tentative heartfelt smile as charming as ever. "Why ever not, when it is for the best," she snapped, setting precedence for distancing herself thus hoping he might see fit to retreat. "Rupert will then be free to wed his heart's desire."

"Where will you go?"

"Devon I think, and if I like it well enough I may seek to rent a property there."

"You are hurting, Estelle, which is only natural," said he, raising her right hand to his lips, a kiss placed thereon. "Do not, my sweet lady, act in haste. My son is a man of honour and will not, God forbid, shirk his responsibilities toward you."

Unaccountable emotions overwhelmed her because he was right. She was hurting, hurting badly, and she dared not tell him why. To put into words the thoughts whirling in her head would weaken her resolve and she could not bear to have his grace or his son pitying her, and yet the duke's every utterance implied sense of sadness at her unbidden misfortune.

She was with child, and never could she bring herself to use a child as a means to forcing Rupert's hand.

"Sleep on what has happened this day and come the morrow perchance you will think upon your friends and how they will feel if you up and abandon them. They have

113

indeed drawn you into their circle with open hearts, and you could not wish for better companions. Rose Davenport's protective gesture toward you earlier was commendable. Be assured Pettigrew observed the way in which she hastened from the carriage and noted how immediate her action in guiding Caroline away from it and into the house. Had he not paid witness to that event I doubt he would have taken it upon himself to inform me that he thought you were as good as hiding in the carriage."

Tears welled and try as she might she could not hold them back. "Can you not see, I do not care if Rupert wants Caroline? He and I were clearly never meant for each other."

"That is the hurt talking, Estelle," said he, letting slip her hands from his grasp. Far from blind, I can see for myself your plight. The signs are all too familiar. I've seen it with my wives and my daughters. "Now do as I say and take early rest this night." With sleight of hand he gently wiped a tumbling tear from her cheek. "Tomorrow you may see your imagination bears blame in causing unnecessary heartache this day."

"I think not and what is more your Grace; you may not be blind to my condition, but you cannot see the truth of Rupert's love for another when it is staring you in the face. You do not see Rupert as others do. You live your life for you."

Aware the carriage had slowed and now turning through the gates of Hazel Grove, he sat back and reached for his gloves. "You are not the first woman to express those sentiments, nor likely to be the last. You see, Estelle, the death of my wife has not only set a fine woman free from a marriage she despised, I am also free to follow my heart and see where it leads." Once again his eyes levelled on hers, his demeanour cold and detached. "I have it in mind to

114

take a grand tour to Vienna, Venice and thence pay visit to a dear friend in Naples. The Countess of Almalfi and I have a great deal in common, the count having passed away a year past."

His words cut as knife cutting flesh for it was his way of saying what a fool he had been to imagine she could ever love him, when such was not wholly true. She had loved him once and perhaps had she never met his son she could have fallen in love all over again.

"I shall take my leave directly," said he, quite matter of fact, as the carriage swung to the left and drew alongside the front entrance, "though I'll not return to Huish Downham at eight miles distant, when Bath is but four."

"Take Rupert's carriage. You cannot possibly ride to Bath in those wet clothes. You may well catch your death."

"If that is my fate then so be it." Jem opened the carriage door and his grace alighted and walked directly to the rear of the carriage. In the brief time taken for her to step down, the stubborn individual had un-tethered his horse, mounted and with a wave of farewell, said, "Be strong, Estelle, and all will be as you want it to be."

With that said he reined away and rode into the night, as wisps of thin cloud scudded past a new moon.

Twelve

City of Bath: Weir Cottage.

Harper seemed exceedingly chirpy on her arrival at his abode, and the outer door left ajar had at first seemed a little odd. But upon hearing him whistling a jaunty tune; she called to him in order to acquaint of her presence and he immediately appeared at the top of the first flight of stairs.

"Come up dear lady, your package awaits collection."

"Oh," said she, ascending and although delighted also a little confused. "I quite thought I had a sitting today."

"Ah well, it so happens there's no call to endure my ugly face peering at you any longer."

He gestured onward and upward to his studio, and whilst brushing past him scent of violets lingered on his person and Harper was no dandy.

"A moment sooner, dear lady, and I might have been somewhat indisposed," said he, a chuckle.

She proceeded ahead of him, amused by his comment for he was well aware of his attraction to the ladies who sought him out and duly commissioned portraits. The strong essence of violets assailing every breath taken suggested one of his more intimate theatrical lady friends had not long vacated the cottage: one of his molls as he referred to his ladies of the stage.

Upon stepping into the attic she was surprised to see a brush discarded with careless abandon to the floor and daub of flesh coloured paint on the bare boards, which implied sense of haste in some matter of great importance to him. He was usually very meticulous with brushes and rarely had she seen a working canvas left uncovered, which he

117

immediately shrouded beneath a blanket. One glance at the chaise longue draped with crimson velvet affirmed one of his molls whom posed for special commissions had lain upon it. Not that she would have ventured to look upon the work in progress. It was simply unavoidably there before her on entering the attic studio.

Harper hastened to a shelf where several small blue velvet pouches concealed miniatures within, and just to be sure he had the right one he let it slide into the palm of his hand. A faint smile flickered and died as he turned to face her, and it was probable he thought her no better than his molls, if truth be told, albeit she did pose with fine silk cloth draped across her person as had Rose.

He replaced the tiny portrait to the velvet pouch, and placed a rather theatrical and dramatic kiss on the pouch. "A beautiful lady I shall miss very much, and I envy the man who will now keep her close to his heart," said he, handing it over.

His words caused a flush to her cheeks, for he knew to whom the miniature was destined. "What can I say, but . . ."

A crash below stairs in keeping with that of crockery breaking and other disturbing sounds stole the moment, for clearly someone had set about wrecking and likely robbing his parlour. He grabbed her shoulders and said all but a whisper, "Stay here, out of sight." And with that he turned and hastened below.

His voice echoed throughout the house upon confronting the intruder, "Damn it. *Why?*"

Silence descended for but a moment and her heart began drumming, fear gripping her, for what followed could not be construed as anything less than a scuffle below her feet. Harper was earnest in protest, his language coarse, and she couldn't tell whether he was winning or losing the fight. His words came forth in breathless bursts amidst the sound of furniture moving and much grunting and groaning. Then silence fell upon the cottage: a deathly silence.

Too afraid to go below she sought a hiding place, unsure whether the silence proclaimed Harper as the victor or the intruder. She knew in her heart there was really nowhere to hide if the intruder had won and had it in mind to search the attic, though perhaps portraits would be of no interest. She tiptoed to life-size canvases leaning against both sides of an overhead beam. The nearest portrait was that of a raven-haired beauty not unlike Caroline though as yet unfinished, who had a skull in one hand and a raven sitting on the other.

On her knees she hurriedly crawled behind it and onward until out of sight, her own portrait standing amidst those awaiting collection. She knew not what to do with hers, for a missive dispatched that very morning would have surely reached Rupert's hands by now and he would have no desire for her portrait adorning any one of his walls.

Aware of footfalls on the stairs she listened; heart in mouth. Was it Harper, if so, why had he not called out declaring all was well? Unable to see who was stalking the attic and whilst terrified and praying for safe deliverance, she listened to the man's feet treading the floor of the studio. It was not Harper. The footfalls were too heavy.

The sudden terrible sound of ripping canvas led her imagination to visualise that of someone slashing a portrait. Oh God, which portrait, and who was this person? A terrible crashing sound implied the frame holding the canvas had either toppled or was dragged from the struts. Was he now satisfied, and his wicked deed concluded? She held her breath, his breathing denoting the exertion of his vile act as he strolled past her position. The sound of crashing pots followed and a paint brush landed inches from her hiding place. What of Harper?

A shadow cast across the gap but momentary, followed by the sound of retreating footfalls suggestive of his taking his leave. She remained motionless, and although relieved to hear feet descending the stairs she could only pray nothing too awful had befallen Harper. And if not for the sound of the outer door slammed shut she would not have dared move from her hiding place.

Her gown dirtied at the knees and pelisse with a cobweb or two attached she emerged and glanced at the tattered portrait lying face down on the floor. It was the one at the far end of the raven-haired beauty. Her only thought was for Harper. She hurried from the attic and rushed down to the parlour, where to her horror she found Harper flat on his back. The table and chairs were toppled and the whole place in a terrible mess. His face looked a sorry mess, too, and copious amount of blood to his artist's smock but not dead, surely not dead?

About to kneel beside him she saw the gash across his throat. He was dead. Bile rose to mouth and she turned and fled and before she could open the main door her stomach heaved and breakfast reappeared.

Whom could she turn to? What of her being there?

Air, she needed fresh air. Needed to think what she must do.

She retreated from the cottage and glanced about her. The terrace was remarkably quiet, though several men were loading flour sacks to a cart outside the mill. A woman who must have passed the cottage moments beforehand carried onward oblivious to her presence: so too a man striding in the opposite direction. She supposed she could scream and thereby draw attention to herself, but what purpose would be gained by it? These unknown persons would ultimately become witnesses to her presence at the cottage whilst Harper was murdered, and the Constable might well perceive such as evidence of her guilt in the horrific manner of his passing.

She walked across the street to the water's edge, the weir before her. Drawing deep breaths she considered her options. She no longer had Rupert's carriage at her disposal, and she knew not where the governess cart would be. After all, a stable hand had brought her to Bath along with her maid, dear Dora with a list of items to purchase and neither expected back at Weir Cottage to collect her until three of afternoon. It was shortly after one of afternoon, therefore two hours before she would set eyes on the maid and groom. She could search the streets and shops all day and not encounter either, and all she wished to do was sit down and cry.

Gathering her thoughts, she reasoned it was not too far to walk to Sydney Gardens and perchance the duke might be at his town house. If not, the resident butler would know how to make contact with the Constable or someone of note within the local militia. Harper's death, terrible though it was, could not have happened at a worse time for his grace. She knew well enough how stressful the days ahead would be, for he had his wife's funeral to arrange, and no doubt half the county would attend the church service. She could easily visualise the vastness of Huish Downham steeped in hushed silence and Pettigrew perpetuating a state of mourning with maids wearing black ribbon bows trailing from their mobcaps and the footmen with black armbands.

Aware she still had the miniature portrait safely in her hand she hurriedly placed it within her velvet drawstring reticule, and hastened onward. At least the miniature would be delivered as agreed to the duke's town house, and in her heart she hoped he might have departed Bath and already en route to Huish Downham. Perhaps the death of the duchess would draw his grace and Rupert closer together, and their differences would finally be resolved.

A pang of guilt suddenly struck her. Sending a letter to Rupert had seemed a cowardly thing to contemplate let alone the wording of it, and she could only live in hope he would understand her reason for doing so. Along with the return of his carriage she had given him no cause to call upon her at Hazel Grove, his belongings within her abode all gathered and neatly packed to a trunk, of which Jem put aboard the carriage albeit with air of reluctance. His words before leaving unforgettable: *'I shall miss you ma'am, for I had it in mind you'd have made for a fine marchioness'*.

In some respects it was a good thing Rose Davenport had let slip the truth about Rupert's love for Caroline, for it allowed her to walk away head held high rather than find herself subjected to the humiliation of Rupert's rejection speech. She doubted not he would have told her face to face how sorry he was, but . . . Well, he wouldn't have to. She had saved him from that indignity.

Turning into the bustle of the main thoroughfare adjacent to Pulteney Bridge she felt far less conspicuous, and within a few moments she was traversing the cobbles of Laura Place. Carriages passing-by tended to draw the eyes of the less fortunate on foot, and it was impossible to remain immune to the elegance of liveried men, horses and the beautifully attired within. Though upon seeing a team of recognisable chestnuts on approach her heart stalled, and she did not wish for Rupert to see her. She turned about in hope his attention was momentarily drawn to the other side of Laura Place, and once the carriage had passed she would then continue on her way.

Heart in mouth she slowed her pace, the team too slowed from trot to walk, which was not so surprising for there seemed to be a commotion on the bridge. There was

122

much shouting, horses neighing and people began rushing forward. A groom leapt from a mail coach followed by the armed guard. Both ran ahead, presumably to offer assistance. Clearly from atop the coach they were afforded full view of a calamity on the bridge, which remained invisible to any one on foot for people had gathered en masse, sense of morbid curiosity prevailing.

She kept walking toward the bridge, not out of need to know what had befallen some poor soul for her action was purely that of avoiding Rupert. Suddenly panic befell the people looking on, many pushing others aside in their haste to escape the path of a runaway horse. With the white's of its eyes visible, froth at its mouth, the stocky grey cob broke through and came onward at a frightening pace with traces and reins trailing in its wake. People pinned themselves to shop fronts and walls and she likewise flattened herself to a wall to allow clear passage as the horse broke into the canter.

Glad to have put distance between herself and Rupert, she had not expected to turn and see him and Jem standing in the path of the petrified horse. Instinct bade her close her eyes but mesmerized she watched as both men held their ground. Surely the horse would trample one of them in its desperate bid to flee the scene, and it was all happening so fast.

Fearing the worst she could not believe it when the horse slowed its pace as though assessing a way to avoid both men. It indeed sought to slip past Rupert who was standing to the far side of the street, Jem standing near to the carriage. Somehow Rupert managed to grab the nearside trailing rein as the animal made to trot past, and although it caused the horse to jolt, the frightened thing gave sway to the hand commanding its bridle and duly lunged round and around its handler in wide sweeping circles. Eventually it tired and the hero of the moment decreased the length of rein and brought the horse to a standstill. Ever the horse lover, no matter its breed, size or colour, Rupert with gloved hand afforded the steaming cob a resounding and reassuring pat to its neck.

A woman in breathless haste came from behind, paused beside her, and said, "Tis a day of miracles, for the horse is unhurt and the child as caused the accident escaped injury, as well. And praise to the *Almighty*, for saving my Bertie." The plump woman drew her woollen shawl tight about herself. "Poor dear came near to heart failure." The woman then rushed onward followed by curious onlookers, her hand raised and calling out to Rupert in grateful manner. "Thank you, thank you, kind Sir, for catching up our Jacko."

By now though, Rupert had handed the horse into Jem's care, and Caroline made her presence known by descending from the carriage to embrace Rupert not caring it was a public arena. Her action and his response could not be construed as less than mutually engaging.

Mildly aware of a man having drawn level, she had not expected the duke to grab her elbow and usher her off the bridge and turn along a narrow alley between houses. "You clearly wish to avoid my son, or you would not have chosen to hang back in the crowd." As soon as shadow fell about them and towering walls on either side reached for the sky, he let slip his grasp on her elbow and caught her hand in his and led onward. "Tradesman's alleyways have their uses."

"Did you see what happened?"

"That of my son's death wish in facing a crazed horse or that of a carter who risked life and limb to prevent a child falling under the hooves of his horse?"

"He did, how?"

"A child ran out from behind its mother's skirts, the carter quick thinking wrenched his horse hard to the right and in doing so his wares slid to the left. The sudden change in weight distribution thus toppled his cart. Luckily he was able to jump clear and his wife sitting on the rear with a boy of twelve years or more equally leapt safe and well to the ground. The horse panicked and the carter sought to release him as soon as able, for the mighty beast was somewhat tangled between shafts, traces and leathers. Unfortunately it broke free of its own accord and took flight."

Having reached the end of the alleyway, the duke turned right along a well-trodden grass and stone path, garden walls either side. She glanced down at her hand still firmly clasped in his, and to her horror his knuckles were reddened and blood on his white cuff suggested . . . Oh God, surely not?

Harper's face came to mind, for he had indeed sustained a terrible beating before the dreadful deed was thus enacted and his life forfeit, and the duke was a man of some strength. But why, why would the duke have cause to murder Harper? She dared not ask, and instead said, "It was fortunate you happened along, and I am most grateful for your knowledge of the alley and this footpath."

"I had no desire to encounter Rupert this day, either."

"It is doubly fortunate for me that you stopped and did not seek to take to the alley unseen, for I was, at that very moment on my way to your town house, and pondering how to get past Rupert without his seeing me."

"I see," said he, glancing her way, though no sign of wariness or guilt. "Then you have the miniature, am I correct?"

"I do, for I came to town for the last sitting earlier today, and Harper had the miniature readied for collection."

"Had I known you were in town we could have taken a turn around the Assembly Rooms and passed a pleasant hour or two, though my face is such a rare sight, perchance we might have drawn attention best not mentioned. After all, I am supposedly a grieving husband. Strange as it may sound, I feel no grief at Constance's passing. I grieved her loss long ago, and we've lived separate lives thereafter. To say I am shocked by the way in which she met with death, yes, indeed, greatly shocked by it."

"Do you suspect foul play as suggested by Lord Brockenbury?"

"Whether I do or not is of little consequence. Needless to say, I cannot summon a soul to mind who would wish her harm." Glancing at her, he drew her hand to his lips. "You do realise if our previous acquaintance came to the notice of the Constable, he might well see cause for a husband ridding himself of a wife in order to marry a mistress."

As he placed a kiss to her fingers, her eyes fell to his cuff. "Are you aware you have blood on your cuff?"

"Damn me, so I have."

"And bruised knuckles," said she, in nonchalant manner to allay any notion she might be thinking him capable of murder.

"That I have and hard-earned in a good cause."

"Good cause?"

"Indeed. The carter needed his cart back on its wheels in order for it to be pushed to the side of the thoroughfare. Along with several gentlemen, the men from the mail coach and other working men we were able to heave it upright. I dare say the carter will reload what he can of his wares and with luck one of the livery stables hereabouts will cobble together enough harness to see his horse and cart reunited for the homeward trek."

126

Relief overcame her, for he had not murdered Harper. "Oh, so you . . ."

He chuckled, part mocking her and part in defence of his honour. "You think as a duke I would not stoop to help a working man?"

"No, because I know you are . . ."

But did she know him at all?

"And that would be?" said he, the end of the path reached, a wider pathway before them.

"You are generous soul, for I do not believe you helped Harper solely for the sake of obtaining a miniature to your personal taste."

He led onward across a carriage ride and halted in line with another alleyway. "We can take this alley, or we can step back to Great Pulteney Street."

"The alley might be best, for I have something I must tell you about Harper."

"Dear God, he didn't . . . didn't approach with indecent proposals?"

"For all of Harper's flirting ways he remained a gentleman throughout my sittings."

This time she led off with the duke keeping pace at a stroll, and he said, "Glad to hear it, for I did wonder at his popularity with the ladies."

"He was most amusing at times, and what has happened is dreadful indeed. I have not told a soul and I am quite scared because I was there at the studio when it happened."

"When what happened?" queried the duke, air of frustration at her lack of clarification of *happened*.

"He's dead. Murdered."

The duke stopped and turned to face her. "You were there? Saw it happen?"

"I saw nothing of Harper's murder. Nor did I see the person who killed him."

"And he died where?"

"In the parlour, whilst I was hiding in the attic."

"Dear God, Estelle," said he, drawing her into his arms. "Had you witnessed his death, I dread to think . . . No, cannot bear to think what might have been your fate."

She hadn't wanted to cry, hadn't wanted to lose control of her emotions, but tears flooded forth. "I couldn't see the murderer. I could only hear him smashing the parlour, and he then attacked a life-size portrait."

"In the attic?"

"Yes."

"Where were you hiding?"

"Between the portraits left leaning against the struts."

He hugged her tight. "Thank God you're here, and unharmed."

"I thank God for that, too."

Easing her from his embrace, he reached into his pocket for a kerchief. "Have you notified the Constable of Harper's demise?"

She mopped her tears. "I had hoped you or your butler would do that for me."

"Then we had best make haste, and dispatch Harris directly to the Constable's office. In the interim we will take tea, and you my dear lady shall then take rest aloft and I'll brook no argument."

"I must return to Weir Cottage by three of afternoon, for a maid and groom will be waiting me there."

"Whilst you're taking rest I shall go to Weir Cottage to see for myself the damage, and be assured I shall see your maid and groom are made aware you are safe with friends." He caught up her hand and they made haste onward, and she thanked his just being there, his voice reassuring. "For a day or two you had best remain at my town house, just to be on the safe side of cautious. We know not who killed

Harper and furthermore, should it become known you were there at the time of the murder no one will know where you are."

Her heart dived. "Oh no, I had not thought of my being there as important. After all, I never set eyes on the brute."

"He may think otherwise if word of your presence reaches his ears, and I have no intention of leaving you exposed and unprotected. You are in my safe keeping until my son comes to his senses and sees the error in letting you slip his grasp."

She and his grace were worlds apart now in his mind, the past very much in the past. His only thought for the future was that of securing happiness for his son, though indeed quite misguided in thinking Rupert was momentarily distracted by Caroline. She dare not tell him Rupert was released from any obligation toward her, and she would not stay in his house a minute longer than necessary.

Thirteen

"Damnable accident." Rantchester brushed himself down, ridding horse hairs from his breeches and sleeve of coat. "It would appear the Pulteney Bridge will remain impassable for some time, what with the wares from the overturned cart still strewn across the main thoroughfare."

"The carter and his wife are doing their level best to return much of it to the now righted cart," said Jem.

Rantchester glanced at the carter's horse, which seemed none the worse for its frightening experience and now walking sedately enough beside the carter's son. "That's our good deed done for the day."

"Aye, and did you 'ear them passengers from the mail coach grumbling amongst themselves. Sounded sore annoyed as they trudged onward on foot."

"The mail coach has no choice but to wait. We on the other hand can turn about."

"And go back to Huish Downham?" said Caroline, indignant in tone.

Whilst Jem held the carriage door, Caroline in vexed manner not unlike the disgruntled passengers of the mail coach hastily scooped up her skirts and marched to the carriage.

"Be reasonable Caroline," said Rantchester, as he followed and then seated himself opposite. "We turn back or we walk to Weir Cottage. Which shall it be?"

"All right, all right, but come the morrow, you shall see how well the portrait is looking."

As Jem closed the carriage door, he said aloud, "Huish it is, then."

"Indeed," snapped Caroline.

131

Rantchester laughed. "Jem was merely relaying directions for Benson, who needs to prepare for taking the horses in a sweeping arc and back the way we came."

She glared in response, unwilling to concede her mistake in thinking Jem's manner as disrespectful to her alone. "That *boy* has an impertinent manner about him."

"Jem is the best groom I've had the good fortune to acquire."

"Then why does he look at me with such disdain? He scowls fit to turn a peachy maid sour to his presence."

"I dare say he became fond of Estelle, and . . ."

"Estelle, Estelle, *Estelle*," said Caroline, livid in tone and expression. "Can we not go a day without your throwing her name my way?"

"Estelle cannot be wiped away as though mere dust on a table. Damn it all, Caroline, I shared a year of my life with her, and likewise Jem and Benson served her as they served me throughout our time together."

"I am all too well aware of that," said she, gripping the seat to steady her balance as the carriage swayed and moved forward, "but you said yourself she wants no more to do with you. And what is more, are you aware she and Captain Finch were lovers before you trotted into her life?"

"You have no need to sully her name, Caroline. It is over between Estelle and I, she made that abundantly clear."

"You say that in one breath and with another express concern for her."

"I *am* concerned about her, for I know her financial situation is not unlike your own."

"And like me she will again find a lover if she sets her mind to it, and perhaps more in keeping with her social standing."

132

He chuckled. "My dearest Caroline, Estelle is fourth cousin to an earl, and you are first cousin to an infamous London whore. You and she are from markedly differing lineage, and God forbid you adopt the very trait my mother despised in others. She duly took you under her wing to spite my father and all he stands for, and it will be said that I have done the same."

"You think I don't know your friends have allied with Estelle, against me. And how do you think I felt when I heard Pettigrew telling his grace he was of mind the Marchioness of Rantchester was sitting outside in your carriage? *Wife*. Of all things your *wife*." Caroline's face bloomed with a pink flush, her ebony eyes daring him to refute her right to state the truth as perceived at the time of eavesdropping at a doorway. "I quite thought I had misheard until your father said he thought it probable in the circumstance of present arrangements within the household. Well, I pondered all but a moment, what circumstance could his grace be referring to? Of course, it then occurred to me, I was, most probably, the circumstance."

Rantchester had known he would tread troubled waters with Caroline. Her nature was unpredictable, her tongue malicious at times, unlike Estelle who had rarely given sway to harsh words. Even now he doubted his sanity for having helped Caroline, albeit he had every intention of breaking loose from her with as little damage inflicted upon Estelle as he could manage. Caroline was lethal and would seek revenge and her kind of revenge would hurt Estelle.

He could not forget Estelle's letter in which she had cast him adrift. To his own fate if truth be told, and guilt had rained down on him whilst reading her kindly words. He was doing ill by Estelle in letting her go, but it was the safest thing to do, for the moment. To say he was clay and Caroline his potter, whom delighted in moulding him to her

133

whims in lascivious manner, and teased him mercilessly with her tongue, such was once the honest truth but not anymore. His wayward nature back then had allowed Caroline to tempt him with baseness all things physical pleasure to the detriment of all else. Love, true love, reached far beyond the heady euphoria of base indulgences, and true love had now slipped his grasp. He was to all intents and purposes falling back into the dark labyrinths of Caroline's madness and her pursuit of bewitching all men to her whims, for it was the only way he could keep her occupied and keep Estelle safe out of Caroline's reach.

"Are you not ashamed at having deceived not only his grace, but the whole household by saying you had wed Estelle?" said Caroline, tearing him from heartfelt regrets. "What did you hope to gain by such a lie?"

"There was no gain to be had from it, for I knew father would rant and rail and likely as not rescind my birthright of passage to the Leighdon fortune."

"You are mad, Rupey, quite mad," said she, leaning forward to place her hand to his knee, "and I can see what attracted you to Estelle. She's fair of face, and not unlike Georgette Lady Brockenbury. I always knew that sweet tongued Georgette held a slice of your heart in her hands, and all the while you treated me as merely a mild distraction to satisfy your carnal desires."

"I was fond of Georgette, true enough, and madness befalls me from time to time as you well know. If such were not the case, I would at this moment be pleading to Estelle's better nature in hope of forgiveness for my mistreatment of her."

Caroline hastily unbuttoned her pelisse, exposing her deliciously plumped bosom for his pleasure, and just as rapidly rid herself of its encumbrance. "Then I must make sure all thoughts of Estelle are banished."

134

Not caring their proximity, the carriage now turned about and starting along Great Pulteney Street, she fell to her knees between his feet in the manner of a whore summoned to his carriage to enact whatever he so desired. With her fingers deft to the concealed fold of his breeches, against his better nature her touch caused instant hardness about him, and it became nigh impossible to deny the pleasure derived from her ministrations. Soon loud groans embodied his gratitude, and Caroline's eyes glittered with intent.

Caught up in the thrill of her daring, one glance through the carriage window proved fatal, for the sight of Estelle and his father the duke, ascending the steps to Grosvenor House, stole the moment. The pleasure in his groin faded, along with imminent euphoria of spending himself in a manner base and degrading for the witch on her knees before him.

His father's hand to the small of Estelle's back implied intimacy, a closeness beyond the measure of mere acquaintance as the pair vanished inside his father's town abode.

When had they become so close?

Caroline's sudden and playful nip to his depleted ardour awakened him to the baseness of her act, and the bite entirely killed his need for release. "Rupey, what ails, today, my sweet? You have me now, as you wanted when I stupidly ran off to marry old Somerville."

There were no words to convey his feelings at the time of Caroline's madness in running off with Somerville. In some respects her going to India had set him free, for he had never loved her, never claimed he had and never would. In like to the opium she had brought into his life and partaken of that very morning, she had long ago initiated him to the delights of physical hedonism unknown before.

135

The combination of both thought and the ultimate hedonistic plain of physical touch, and God forgive his weakness, the softness of Caroline's lips pressed to him, embracing him, reignited his former ardour, and her insistence of drawing the life-force from his loins served to quell his racing mind. He was momentarily slave to her whim and she would take all of him, and drag him through *Hell*, his senses striving for nuance of imminent *Heaven*.

Try as he might to desist in her salacious attentions and regain sense of his worth and honour, the ultimate welled in potency. In need of breath, his moment of gratification upon him, the delight in her eyes expressed satisfaction in knowing she had led him to consummate bliss, and he knew her words would be as taunting as ever once he was spent and she having drunk him dry.

"You see, Rupey," said she, triumphal air about her, "we were meant for each other, for in my short married life dear old Somerville never set me alight in wantonness to adore his cock as I do yours."

"Happen not," said he, well aware of man's needs at the expense of their womenfolk. His own past lay littered with brief encounters not unlike their present engagement save the presence of opium and that of heightened sensual awareness, "but I dare say your carriage antics brought him close to heart failure on occasion of your lascivious behaviour."

She scrambled back to the seat opposite, her tone icy. "I had no choice in the matter of pleasing my husband, though will say this for him. He devoured me in like manner, long before I mounted him." She raised her chin in haughty manner, air of extreme annoyance. "Unlike you, of whom I have not ridden since my return. Nor you of I, and if you keep me waiting much longer I shall flirt with your father."

Hastening to redress his fast depleting appendage, his thoughts drifted to Estelle, and the gentle and loving way she had responded to mutual affections besides that of full couplings, of which they had indulged throughout their year together in sensual harmony. Had he instigated a similar scenario to that just enacted, and Estelle the victim of his tongue, she might have obliged in riding him to the trot within the carriage.

"Are you thinking about that woman, again?"

"Not at all," fibbed he, a chuckle. "Why would I, when I have a woman such as you to tempt me beyond all consideration of begetting a wife."

She threw her reticule at him, catching him full face. "If you think to keep me as your mistress, I shall not be as compliant as Estelle. You shall not make a fool of me as you did of that misguided strumpet."

"Strumpet she is not," he said, defensive of Estelle, "and had my mother met her, I am now convinced she would have had us wed as soon as could be arranged."

"Pah, it was your mother's wish that you and I should get wed."

"In that she cannot agree nor deny your claim."

"Oh Rupey, I am so sorry, so sorry. I should not have mentioned your mother in this sad time of your grieving."

"Apology accepted."

Caroline cast her eyes to the window and silence befell them, and blaming Estelle's letter for his action of surrendering to the vixen seated across from him afforded no excuse for his weakness. The letter had expressed nothing but love and compassion for his loss and, Estelle had wished him well for the future. There was no mention of Caroline, save to say she hoped all would be well and happiness would reign. But why the letter, and what had suddenly caused Estelle to set him adrift?

The vision of his father and Estelle in intimate discourse then leapt to mind, as did the severed girth of his mother's saddle. There was no possible link between the two events: *how could there be*?

His father had despised the very idea of his son contemplating marriage with *'that woman'* and yet a few moments ago the Duke of Leighdon and Estelle had seemed utterly at ease in each other's company.

Had he misread intimacy between them before, in the library at Huish Downham?

Dear God, he had no desire to think badly of Estelle. And yet, his father had admitted to having a mistress. He glanced at Caroline, her sultry beauty undeniable and Somerville, a man twenty-two years her senior who'd adored her.

Was it possible something had sparked between Estelle and his father?

At Huish Downham something strange had occurred that day in the library, his father's genial spirit much at odds with his former railing stance of *'that woman'* shall not step across the threshold. *Damn it, why could he not see it*? *Where lay the clues*? But of course, the very day of his mother's tragic accident Estelle came to the house and remained in the carriage. Shortly afterwards it became apparent his father had departed on horseback despite heavy rains. *'To Bath on business Pettigrew'* had said. *Why then had his father not journeyed by coach*?

Deception and betrayal seemed as though on the wind and not an ounce of proof did he possess to hand. Heart beating, pulse racing, anger welled and there was only one way to quell his curiosity. He would ride over to Hazel Grove first thing in the morning and face up to his mistreatment of Estelle. If she refused to see him, he would

138

glean what he could from servants, and act accordingly to secure she was never wanting in any way.

Fourteen

Hazel Grove.

He may yet need to beg her forgiveness, and whilst on approach to Estelle's residence Rantchester blessed Caroline's desire to have a risqué portrait of her charms adorning her bedchamber: *'As soon as might be arranged'* her parting shot. For despatched to Weir Cottage for her last sitting and to arrange collection of her portrait in due course, albeit under protest, she had nevertheless conceded business to do with his mother's funeral called for his attention. He in turn had said: *'The cost of a portrait was a small price to pay in exchange for her devotion to imaginative pleasures of the flesh',* of which, to his shame he had indulged a day past, thus she had left with a big smile on her face and he free to do as he wished.

He had several hours before Caroline would again set foot inside Huish, and more than time enough to appease Estelle in attempt to redeem his unforgivable behaviour in paying court to Caroline, presupposing his heart's desire would deign to give him audience. There was no going back on what he had done the day of yesterday, and he could not hate himself any more than he already did, nor did he expect Estelle to welcome him with less than sense of coldness and detachment.

Hazel Grove was now in sight, its low slung frontage daubed with the last vestiges of summer lingering as vivid red and yellow roses rambled up and over windows. He duly reined his horse from trot to the walk, and braced himself for outright rebuttal. Damn it to hell, she had every

141

right to demand he turn about and never set a foot, his horse or wheels through the main gateway ever again.

A lad hared from the stable yard, his grimy face akin to that of a street urchin and as bold in brass tongue. "Sir, we been a wondering where you was, 'cause the mistress 'ave disappeared."

His heart sank, incredulity hitting him squarely on the jaw as good as any punch. "By that you mean?"

"What I said," replied the lad, genuine in his concern and forthright with it. "She never came home of yesterday, and none of us do know where she is."

Lost for words, his thoughts drifted to the image of Estelle and his father.

"It all be very strange," said the lad, glaring up at him as though the man before him was the cause of Estelle's disappearance, "her vanishing like that and the artist murdered."

"Harper, murdered?"

"According to Molly and Jewkes he were dead. They went to collect the mistress at three of afternoon from Weir Terrace a day past, and the Constable weren't letting a soul near the artist's house, 'cause there were valuable portraits inside. 'Twas a gentleman, who 'twas thought was your father the duke, who did tell Molly as how the mistress was safe with friends. He told Molly to pack a trunk for her mistress and that he would send someone to collect it this afternoon."

"Did he indeed, and no word of where the trunk was destined for?"

"No, Sir."

Glad that he hadn't dismounted he reined Huntsman about, the lad quick to step away. "God bless you Sir, and pray you find her."

"That I will."

Estelle glanced at the clock on the mantelshelf. It was two of afternoon, and feeling trapped and isolated in the duke's vast town house, she strolled to the bedchamber window; Sydney Gardens before her. She could fully understand why the duke had turned to this house as a sanctuary from the stresses incurred at Huish Downham, the very place in which he had claimed he never felt able to relax as he should in his own house.

Despite the passing of carriages and people walking in the municipal gardens there was a defined tranquillity about the locale akin to that of a less formal village atmosphere. It was so unlike the bustle of the city centre and the formal promenading at the Assembly Rooms. Within the house too, as seen the day prior, Harris and the duke retained sense of reasonable formality between them appropriate to manservant and duke, and yet a distinct air of friendship. She had not seen that same sense of familiarity at Huish Downham betwixt the duke and Pettigrew. But perhaps Pettigrew's allegiance was more inclined toward the late duchess, which was readily understandable due to the duke's long absences from the house. But she must forget about the duke's estate and all that it entailed, her link with Rupert was lost and gone forever.

Her eyes again fell on Sydney Gardens. If only she could take a stroll across the green and walk beneath the trees, for it embodied sense of the countryside, and yet itself within walking distance of the hub of society.

The duke had as good as forbidden any notion of her setting foot outside the house unescorted, and she had agreed to abide to his advice. After all a murderer was out there, somewhere, and she could so easily become his next victim.

She had indeed felt safe knowing his grace was in the house overnight, and since his setting off for Huish Downham loneliness had befallen her, for it was imperative he return to his estate. His wife's funeral was Thursday next, but two days hence, and it was suggested she should attend. He could see no reason for her absence, and had stated *'it was time Rupert faced her as a man should'*. Though both had agreed over dinner, the night previous, she and Rupert were simply not meant to be. Furthermore, she had made it quite clear she had no wish to cause Rupert any discomfort, nor did she bear ill-will toward him.

The duke undeterred by her reluctance to show face at his country abode had insisted her presence would please him. So it was her fate to await the duke's carriage to convey her to Huish Downham or break her promise and slip from the house when Harris was otherwise detained below stairs and out of sight of the main entrance door.

She would soon have a change of clothes for the duke's carriage was destined to collect a trunk of clothing and personal effects from Hazel Grove, not a word of its intended destination to be revealed to her servants. Poor Molly and her personal maid Dora were probably quite distraught by now and pondering their mistress' fate.

One more night at the duke's house and Harris might be less inclined toward knocking at doors to see if she required anything, which was essentially his way of guarding her from harm. But what harm could befall her when the outer doors were all bolted? And the sooner she could get back to Hazel Grove, the better. The same level of security could readily be applied to the house. It also had the advantage of remoteness and perchance too far distant for the murderer to venture.

Yes, it was quite feasible to slip from the house albeit a little risqué. She could then call at a nearby coaching yard where private drags could be hired. Oh, but monies. She snatched at her reticule discarded on the window seat, and hurriedly glanced inside. She then remembered she had but sixpence, a halfpenny and a farthing, and all due to Molly shopping with three guineas the day prior. Any money left over was now at Hazel Grove. There was nothing for it but to secure sufficient monies from a bank, of which she was loath to do. How ironic it all was, for her trust account was held at the Grosvenor Bank, owned by his grace.

Movement outside drew her attention to the street below, and of all people it had to be Rupert dismounting from the Huntsman. As always impeccably dressed, and today in a dark blue overcoat he looked as dashing as ever. Her heart blipped, trepidation befalling her. True enough her feelings toward him had fallen to confused state of not knowing her heart at all. The duke's presence the day and evening prior, although reassuring in a fatherly way the spark that had once burned between them had seemingly vanished. And now to her chagrin Rupert stirred a burning desire she thought never to experience again upon seeing him.

She stepped back from the window half fearing he might have caught sight of her whilst on approach. How silly. She had no reason to fear him, though discourse between them might be a tad awkward and no doubt long pauses would ensue.

Bracing herself she expected the inevitable tap at the door and that of Harris announcing the Marquis of Rantchester's presence, for in normal circumstances Rupert would be unlikely to tug the bell-pull and wait for Harris to open the door. He would enter of his own volition.

The bell clanged incessantly.

She waited, and waited, and waited, but silence reigned throughout the house. Sidling closer to the window again she glanced down to see Rupert remounting the Huntsman; *but why, and why did his presence stir her heart so*? She watched as he rode away and disappeared from view, and to her dismay tears tumbled forth. She hastily dabbed them away with a kerchief well aware her life was crumbling from around her. All her hopes and dreams were lost because Caroline Somerville had walked back into Rupert's life.

All but a few moments, and a tap at the door declared Harris, whom she bade enter, his face a picture of triumph.

"The Marquis enquired as to why the outer door was bolted. I informed him his father departed for Huish Downham soon after breakfast, and it suited my purpose to bolt the door whilst I went down to the cellar. He grudgingly accepted I had forgotten to unbolt it again. He then asked if a lady guest might be staying in this house. I lied, and pray God forgive me for I have not fibbed since childhood when held to account for a broken window of which I vociferously denied any hand in its destruction. To be quite frank, ma'am I don't think the marquis believed me."

"He departed nonetheless, when he could so easily have entered and made life somewhat difficult for us."

"There is no livery yard close at hand, and I have never known the marquis to leave his horse tethered outside this house for more than a minute or two."

"Yes, he does prize the Huntsman, greatly."

"He was no doubt en route to his Royal Crescent abode

where abides a young lad who will lead the Huntsman to the nearby mews." Harris drew breath, concern etched on his face. "The marquis may yet return here on foot, which is not so unusual."

"I see, but in all honesty he is no threat to me."

"No ma'am. On the other hand, the duke has much to contend with at present, for it would seem there is an element of mystery surrounding the death of the duchess." Harris cleared his throat, air of nervousness perhaps in broaching the duke's private matters. "Your presence in this house, ma'am, could prove embarrassing for him should events turn for the worse."

"Turn for the worse . . . How so?"

"I'm no Constable, nor am I a lawyer, but I am of mind if the Constable witnessed what I've witnessed with mine own eyes in this house, it could well condemn his grace in the eyes of the law. I cannot and will not deny your innocence in accepting the duke's protection in your time of need, but I fear his regard for your safety may do him ill."

"His regard is but that of a dear friend."

"No ma'am, it is out of love that he protects you, a love that knows no bounds for those he regards as family. When his grace returns to his London residence it is I who will travel ahead to forewarn his household staff of his imminent arrival, and there I shall remain to attend upon him. To say I am aware of his . . . How shall I say . . . A lady friend of a year past, well, it ended badly for the duke and he swore he would never make the same mistake again."

So Harris knew the duke had indeed had a lady friend in London, and knew of the severed girth strap on the duchess' saddle. Freddie Davenport's words on the day of the duchess' death suddenly leapt to mind: *'It's not as if the duke has a mistress hidden away, for such could be construed as evidence of his wanting rid of his wife'.*

Dear God, if her presence at Beckford Road became common knowledge the duke would be damned. "I cannot stay here, Harris, for if you are right in your belief, then many aspects of my presence here could be misconstrued. I must return to Hazel Grove."

Harris let slip a compassionate smile. "Indeed ma'am. And in all honesty I see no other way of saving his grace from himself, for the moment that is. If you feel able, then I am willing to escort you home."

"I must take leave as soon as can be arranged, for I have no monies of any great value with me. Do you think it safe for me to go to the bank? Once I am home. From there I shall with my valued servants take leave from Somerset in a matter of days, if not hours."

"No ma'am, it is far from safe for you to venture abroad of the streets. It therefore falls to me to engage the services of a private drag to get you safely to Hazel Grove, and I have monies aplenty gratis his grace for housekeeping." He turned, paused, a tentative smile. "I shall away to the livery yard, and if the duke's coachman is running to clock-work time your trunk will be here by four at the very latest. Five of evening would be a good time to take our leave from here."

"You know best, Harris. I am utterly in your hands."

"Ah well, I have it in mind the marquis will return here at a round six in time for supper at eight, his aim to catch us unawares."

"What of supper?"

"The marquis will eat alone."

With that said, Harris departed and closed the door, and confusion befell her. Her heart had told her to set Rupert free on hearing Rose Davenport's story of his disastrous

148

affair with Caroline: for the woman's hold on his heart was seemingly as strong as ever. Freddie had as good as said she should fight for Rupert, and cast Caroline to the four winds. The duke too, had said he hoped Rupert would come to his senses and not let her, Estelle, escape his clutches. And she, who had foolishly thought the duke held her close to his heart when his affection was but fatherly and caring toward her. She now had no one who cared for or about her beyond seeing her safe until the murderer was apprehended, if ever.

Lady Fate had dealt a cruel hand in so many ways. *But what of the portrait slashed to ribbons by Harper's murderer? Was the dark mysterious lady, indeed Caroline?*

Fifteen

Time marched, thus the clock on the mantle began to chime just as the duke's black coach rolled to a halt outside Grosvenor House: precisely on the fourth hour of afternoon, the family crest emblazoned on its claret coloured doors.

She studied the four-in-hand; a team of magnificent dapple greys standing below in the street. They were indeed, a sight not to be missed. She nonetheless kept to the shadows whilst watching the groom offloading her trunk. His green greatcoat trimmed with gold braid was very smart and his highly polished brown boots immaculate; his hat all the while shielding his face from view. He carried the trunk to the door with admirable ease implying great strength of back and arms.

Harris had already asked a maid to remain in the hallway in order to slip the bolts and allow entry to the groom, just in case Harris himself incurred delay at the coaching inn. As yet Harris had not returned, and the maid's voice and a manly chuckle in the hallway echoed from below, implying the maid and groom were like as not well acquainted or a little flirting was afoot.

It was not long before a manservant intervened, his earnest deliberation quite curt in manner.

"The trunk is delivered, and best you get on your way, my man."

"Aye, laddie. So I shall, when I know what time the coach is expected back here on the morrow."

"It's not your place to question when your services will be required," said the manservant. "Mr. Harris will send word to the mews first thing."

"Can yee not see my reason, laddie, for if the carriage is expected here ten-minutes afore the passenger is in wont to depart for Huish that is mean preparation time for the likes of us?"

Listening to the groom putting forth a reasonable request she felt she should step forth and order the carriage returned to Huish immediately, and indeed state she had no need of it. But if she did, she would need some sort of explanation for the duke.

The groom was a persistent fellow. "Can you not ask?"

"Ask whom?" challenged the manservant.

"Whomever that ruddy trunk belongs to," snarled the groom, "and you can *man* me all you want, but while you were still wetting your pants I was fighting Bonaparte at Waterloo. Now damn well find out what time that carriage out there is required on the morrow."

The air of authority in the groom's voice spoke of rank, his voice suddenly very succinct and barely a hint of dialect from north of the border as heard beforehand. Who was this fellow, and why so aggressive in manner?

"You're new at this," said the manservant, "and new at Huish no doubt, lest you would know servants don't question orders nor demand orders to suit their fancy any more than a soldier would give orders to officers."

"Fancy be damned," said the groom, "for the horses need harnessing, the coach needs hitching and the mews are what . . . a quarter-hour distant from here, according to Cyril. And with just two of us and a team of four that's a half-hour at best in getting ready to depart the mews; the horses groomed 'n' all."

She could bear it no longer and hastened from the room and descended the staircase. The groom was far older than imagined at close quarter, a patch shielding his left eye. His build was slim and yet broad of shoulder, his hair as grey as black, his face weathered, bearded and tanned, and his one good hazel coloured eye veered her way as keen as any bird of prey.

He removed his hat, tucked it underarm and bowed in military manner. "Ma'am," said he, "may I enquire as to the time you will require the coach brought to the house on the morrow?"

She would be lying whatever time she put forth, but said, "Half-past eleven." He held her gaze and she visualised a man of high military rank masquerading below his station for there was something faintly familiar about him, and she asked, "And to whom am I speaking?"

"Braithwaite, ma'am." Without waiting to be dismissed he turned and strode to the entrance door as though eager to depart: his footfalls heavy and echoing throughout the hallway. He then paused, and furthered, "From north of the border."

With that he closed the door behind himself.

The lean youthful manservant winked at the maid in a reassuring way. She in turn flashed a fleeting smile at him, as he said, "Shall we take the trunk aloft, ma'am?"

"Yes, please do," said she, her thoughts dwelling on the man *from north of the border*, whilst the pair hefted the trunk from the floor and hurried on their way.

The groom's leave taking had seemed purposefully discourteous as though intended to impart some meaning, though to what objective she couldn't imagine. She dreaded to think what his reaction would be when word reached the mews ordering the duke's coach back to Huish.

Whilst hurrying back to the drawing room and suddenly as though marching in time to the groom's footfalls departing Grosvenor House, she recalled the murderer's footfalls stomping across Harper's attic. But no, it could not be the same man. Huish was too far distant from Bath for the groom to be in two places at once. All the same, something about him had seemed odd, odd indeed, and familiar.

She hurried to the window to see the coach setting off from the house and to her relief spied Harris on approach. He acknowledged the coachman with raised hand in passing and likewise the coachman returned the gesture. The groom on the other hand merely cast a glance over his shoulder, and whether his intention was to familiarise himself with Harris or to see if she might be looking on she could not be sure. She had a notion it was the latter, but why? What possible interest could he have in her, unless . . . unless he had known her father or her husband. Perhaps he had it in mind they had met before and he was no more able to recall when or where such might have occurred than she could.

It was but a moment or two before Harris tapped the door and stepped into the drawing room minus his outdoor coat and hat. "It is all arranged, ma'am. We leave at five."

"Thank you so very much, Harris, and I shall reimburse your expenses as soon as we reach Hazel Grove."

He cast a smile. "I shall be happy enough to see you safe at home and away from the city, for rumours are rife about Harper and his gambling debts. It seems he had some unsavoury friends, more enemies than friends if you get my meaning. One of his theatrical lady friends was fished out of the river this morning downstream from the weir. It was said she might have been there a couple of days, but nobody knows for sure. There was quite a rumpus at his house today, as well. A Lady Caroline acting more akin to a trollop was heard shouting at the militiamen about a portrait inside the house and she demanded the soldiers hand it over. Well, apparently they let her go inside so they would know which one to bring out, and it was gone."

So it *was* Caroline's portrait. "Gone? But I saw it. It was shredded."

Harris looked astounded. "You saw it?"

"I did, and I too have a portrait awaiting collection."

"Leave that to me, and I shall have it delivered to Hazel Grove within the week."

"You are so very kind, Harris."

"No trouble, ma'am, no trouble at all." He cast a kindly smile. "Will you take tea, now?"

"Yes Harris, I will. A calming tea may instil a little courage for the journey ahead. First though, I simply must change to clothing more suited to the chills of an eventide ride."

He stepped aside allowing exit from the room. "Tea in ten-minutes, ma'am?"

"On the dot," said she, hastening to her bedchamber, glad in her heart to know she would soon be safe at Hazel Grove.

Instinct bade Ranchester return to Grosvenor House, thus he stepped from his house in the *Royal Crescent* and turned left, his strides fast covering the sweeping arc of the roadway. Refreshed and re-dressed after his ride from Huish he had it in mind to call on Ranulph Brockenbury before once again descending unannounced at Grosvenor House: at around six of evening.

Absolutely convinced Estelle was there despite Harris having said otherwise, he was satisfied she was safe for now and out of harm's way.

On turning into Brock Street a commotion outside the house he had oft frequented in moments of dire need, gave rise to concern. Soldiers of the Militia were dragging people forth and bundling them onto a wagon no matter their rank in society; all the while whores were yelling abuse at the soldiers.

Whilst the part-dressed whores were left sitting alongside dishevelled hastily dressed gentlemen, he thanked the *Almighty* such had never occurred whilst he was inside that house partaking of the pleasures to be gained from the dream smoke. And to be caught with a whore ministering to his pleasure in like to Caroline's favoured way of setting him alight, a worse scenario he could not imagine.

Those standing looking on and passing by would soon spread the word about the whoring gentlemen, and there were going to be a few red-faces yet to appear before wives in the aftermath of such a calamity.

He dodged past bystanders and stepped to the other side of the street his heart going out to the men who were obviously caught with their breeches about their knees by the Constable, and all within a place that was to the outside world a mere private gentleman's club. He thanked the *Almighty* again, because the whores were so intent on giving the soldiers a rough verbal dressing down and naming those they themselves had serviced that he slipped by unnoticed and unchallenged by any the painted ladies.

Damn it he was a lucky fellow. In all the years he had frequented the club nothing had ever brought the Constable to the door with a platoon of militia at his back. *What in the deuce had happened to bring the wrath of the law to this place?* To the casual eye the building was no different than any of the houses along the thoroughfare, the door likewise attended to by a footman.

As he passed onward a man with a patch over one eye was suddenly hauled from the house, and the fellow was putting up a concerted effort to slip the grasp of two soldiers. How it happened he couldn't say, but the man broke free with one arm and the soldier to his right disappeared from view: wrestled to the ground and no doubt senseless. The second soldier suffered the same indignity and the assailant with brutal force shoved the Constable out of his way and took flight at a fast run toward the *Crescent*.

The Constable shouted for the soldiers to apprehend the man or shoot the blighter. A soldier at the rear of the wagon fired a shot and missed his target. The one-eyed man then vanished around the corner of the house. Two soldiers ran after the escapee whilst the Constable and the remaining soldiers contended with whores who as opportunist as ever had leapt from the wagon and were fleeing in all directions.

Standing on Ranulph's doorstep he changed his mind about paying visit and walked onward. The sooner he stepped across the threshold of Grosvenor House the sooner he could lay his case before Estelle. She was there; he would lay his life on that bet.

To hell with Caroline, he wanted Estelle.

Sixteen

Huish Downham.

Damn it, life had cruel twists and turns, even for a duke.

Ensconced in the library he reached for a glass of brandy, his thoughts whirling in a maelstrom of concern over his son's seeming abandonment of Estelle, for there was no hope of his stepping into his son's shoes. Estelle was out of his reach, her heart Rupert's.

Could his life become any more damn complicated than at present? God he hoped not, and yet events had made it quite clear the girth attached to his late wife's saddle had been slashed with intent to cause injury or death to the rider. Who had done such a dreadful thing and why, baffled him.

Whilst quaffing at his brandy, the mess at Harper's studio kept leaping to mind. Again another murder and neither he or the Constable could see reason enough to suspect the murders were in any way related. The slashed portrait was righted and they both witnessed the image thereon, and agreed it must have had some bearing on Harper's death. And yet, Caroline's portrait could merely have been in the wrong place at the wrong moment. Albeit her face had survived attack of blade to canvas, the rest of her was rendered to little more than strips of canvas trailing from the framework not unlike flesh dangling from a body.

The Constable had put forth a plausible scenario as to how Constance was never the intended victim of the slashed girth, but neither could fathom why anyone would wish to harm Caroline. Again, it was a complete mystery. He could think of several women who had cause enough to

159

despise Caroline Lady Somerville, not least Estelle. None of the women to his knowledge were brave enough to kill Caroline in brutal manner. A soup made with poisoned mushrooms, deadly nightshade and digitalis, yes, by far more in keeping with the ladies of the district who might dream of smiting Caroline: merely a dream nonetheless.

He was sure Constance had met with her untimely death due to some other reason, regardless of the fact one or two ladies of mean eye were present in the stable mews prior to the hunt, and may have heard Caroline would be riding the duchess' favoured horse.

He checked his pocket-watch its fob chain slithering between his fingers. It was five-minutes past the seventh hour, dinner due at eight and here he was downing brandy before due time. Damn it to hell his life had turned a corner he had so badly wanted but never at the expense of Constance losing her life. And yes, he had wanted Estelle but not like this, and she was now beyond his reach. Her heart he knew belonged to Rupert and pray to *Heaven* his son would come to his senses before long. If not he would himself feel duty bound to provide for Estelle if but from a safe distance.

The door suddenly burst open and there stood Caroline; her plumped bosom heaving with every breath drawn, a ravishing red silk gown shimmering as though set aflame. "Where is Rupert?" she screamed, advancing toward him as though it was his fault his son was absent. "I returned from Bath hours ago and still he has not come back from his ride. What possible reason could he have for staying away for so long?"

Where manners bade him rise in the presence of a lady he had no compulsion to oblige Caroline. Nor would he have her flaunting herself before him as though she was now the duchess in residence. Even if he knew where

Rupert was he would be loath to tell her. If nothing else he could stir dissent and happen she might leave Huish of her volition.

"Has it not occurred to you he has a duty to Estelle regardless of his friendship with you," said he, having already warned Rupert to the effect he had best have a word with Estelle, though no mention as to why. "He is after all, the least inclined to abandon his friends, let alone a mistress he has fallen in love with."

"To her, why would he go to her?" seethed the voluptuous young strumpet before him. "She sent him a letter setting him free from any obligation toward her."

"Perhaps so . . ."

"Not a perhaps," said she, cutting him mid-flow. "I saw the letter with mine own eyes. She wants no more of him."

"And you think that letter will stop him loving her? For with mine own eyes I have witnessed the way his eyes devour Estelle. She holds his heart as no one has held it before, nor likely to in the future."

"Pah, you see only what you want to see. I know my Rupey. We are made for each other."

"Rupert is not as easily swayed by your salacious nature, as happened in the past."

"You think not?" said she, her dark eyes daring him to refute her claim on Rupert's lustful nature. "And you, your grace, are you utterly immune to my charms?"

He placed his glass on the desk and gained his feet glaring down at her. She was every bit the vixen in red, her dark sultry features appealing in a way he had never looked upon her before. *Was it the brandy fogging his brain, the red of her gown or the bareness of her shoulders and the curve of her breasts?* Dear God, he could be tempted, sorely tempted to teach her a lesson she deserved.

161

She moved around the desk coming closer, hands on hips and lips pouting in the manner of a recalcitrant child hell-bent on making life difficult for any adult who posed authority over her. "Ah ha, I do believe silence dictates you like what you see," said she.

He wagered if he made a move on her she would turn about and flee and lock herself in her room and leave him in peace to enjoy his dinner alone. "What I see is a teasing wench who craves attention. One who will resort to almost any damn means at her disposal to bring a man to his knees before her."

"And I see a man of considerable handsomeness standing before me. A man of vigour as witnessed when out hunting. A man who would have me on my knees before him, unlike Estelle, is that not so?"

The damn vixen was too observant. "Any pretty young thing deserves an appreciative male eye, and you my lady, are you not given to appreciation from men?" Whether it was too much brandy and empty stomach or madness, he reached for her, his arm coiling about her waist, but there was no struggle, no determined effort to escape his clutches. As he drew her close his intent was to scare her off, but her hand went straight to his crotch seeking manly arousal.

"We are alone, and what is more your *Grace*, your need is as great as mine." She was a vixen indeed and deft in releasing a man's appendage, her fingers exploring his fast burgeoning mass. Without a hint of shame she was taking the lead, and on tiptoe she brushed her lips across his in teasing manner. "Does that not please your Grace?"

Dear God, he was long overdue in satisfying inner needs in a gratifying manner. She was as he had always thought, an opportunist harlot; her hand caressing his manliness and tongue dancing on his lips in the manner of a temptress. He

162

could cease her tormenting touch with icy words and dismiss her from his company, but her fondling was nonetheless as overtly pleasing to the senses as essence of rose water permeating his nostrils.

The cut of her gown gave sway to sliding from her left upper shoulder with ease, a breast duly bared for his delighting and amply filling his hand. A moan escaped her lips declaring pleasure at his touch. Likewise her fingers clasped tightly around his hardened self to pleasure him further, but the game she might be playing intrigued him.

"Why me?" he said, unwilling to engage in momentary tease and then find himself left in pained lustful hardness.

"Why not?" said she, unabashed whilst caressing his swollen manly appendage with zeal, "for I have my needs and Rupert is wilful in neglect and we are alone, your Grace."

The softness of her flesh and a rosy nipple budding between his fingers brought forth sweet memories of similar moments from his past. "In what manner would you have me oblige your neglected self, if I agree to this encounter proceeding further?"

She suddenly let fall her grip on him, and said, "Sit down, your Grace, like a good boy, and I will demonstrate my needs. Your chair will suffice. It is amply big enough for two people to engage as one."

He sat back in his chair half expecting she would flee giggling like a wicked tease or cackling like an evil witch. She did neither and stepped toward him, hauled up her gown, and the base delight in seeing the cleft beneath her dark silken mound set his heart racing. The need to touch overwhelmed him, and he savoured the moment of gliding his hand between her legs, of dragging his fingers up through the cleft of her, and of stroking her nub and seeking the moisture of aroused woman from within. It was so long

163

since the pleasures of a young woman had fallen to his hands, a woman as blatant as Caroline. He was past the point of turning her away. He had to have her, had to sate a slow burning ache in his groin.

"Come now, your Grace," said she, placing her left foot to the right side of his seat, "you do want me, do you not?"

What else but sheathing his hardened self within her would satisfy his growing need, her hands deployed to keeping her skirts aloft pleased the eye. He slipped his hands beneath her bunched skirts and cupped her mooned rump forcing her cleft to his mouth. Fresh from a bathing tub, all sweet and delicious he savoured her sex flesh, his tongue dabbling and diving and her soft moans music to his ears. It was madness, utter madness to have fallen foul to the young vixen and there was no going back. No stepping away from the gratification to be gained from this harlot. She was every bit a lethal young lady well-versed in provocative words to lead a man astray, and her body finally falling to trembles and shudders of womanly release could not be wasted. She would not escape him if that be her plan. It was too late. He would have his way with her now, even if he had to blackmail the ultimate from her.

"You are a wicked man, your Grace," said she, sliding knees either side and straddling him: thence seating herself astride him.

Breathless, her breasts heaving and wantonly desirous to engage in mutual pleasure, she had by her own action negated need of his taking her by foul means. Words were superfluous whilst she deftly guided his hardness to her cleft. The sheer joy of having her slide onto him, sheathing him stole his breath. Too long . . . it had been too long since a woman had sat astride him and delighted in his rigid muscle pleasuring her with slow sensual lovemaking. God,

164

how he had longed to indulge such pleasure with Estelle and always she had denied him.

Caroline was a harlot and nothing about her imparted loving tenderness. She was riding him hard and fast just as she rode horses in cruel manner: one leg deliciously hooked around a horn, the other stretched with foot to stirrup, her whip vicious to the hind quarters of her mount. The pain of her need and the pleasure of it all caused his heart to drum in his chest. He was giving sway to base lust, keening the ultimate sensation and willing it ever onward but it was eluding him. Damn it the harlot had wanted him, had needed him, and she was satisfying a need he had long hoped would be quelled by Estelle.

Dear God, Estelle. A mere glimpse of that fair lady's cleft had brought him to his knees only to be denied the pleasure of sinking his hardness within her. But she was here now, in his thoughts, her luscious loins wrapped around him. He was sheathed within her, and with one almighty upward thrust he spent himself, the agony and ecstasy as real as though it was indeed Estelle astride him.

Caroline's moans and sighs in the throes of womanly orgasm proclaimed his age had no bearing on his ability to still pleasure a woman with the fullness of his cock alone. He drew much needed breath, his heart pounding his hardness pulsing. Happen the Countess of Amalfi would lust his company in the not too distant future.

"Your *Grace*," exclaimed Caroline, seeming a tad unwilling to slip from his lap as though savouring the last vestiges of his rigid muscle pulsing in time to the thunder of his heart. "You satisfy a woman exceedingly well." She leaned forward breasts exposed and feathered her lips across his. "We must engage again, soon, very soon."

Although spent and stomach rumbling in want of food,

her breasts were delightful and he could not help but fondle one last time. He was most definitely beyond redemption this night, and happen as not would oblige Caroline again if tempted beyond resistance. Curious as to how sincere she was in accommodating the master of the house, he asked, "And Rupert, what shall you do about my son?"

"If I have you, what need have I for Rupert? Your tongue delights as his never has."

"We keep any future liaisons secret, do you understand, secret?"

"But of course, and perchance you will find you cannot do without me."

Ha, the wicked young madam had it in mind to drive him insane and thereby lusting after her, and he then foolish enough to make her his duchess. A rude awakening awaited Caroline Somerville if that was her aim, and a little generosity and guile would no doubt see her on her way to Scotland sooner than she had intended, with gifts aplenty in exchange for her favours.

"You are undressed, Lady Vixen, and dinner is nigh."

She lunged away from him in youthful almost childlike haste, her new title seeming to please her. "Would it be improper to pay visit to your bedchamber at the midnight hour?

She beamed a smile, a wicked spark of intent within her eyes whilst rearranging her bodice. He likewise hastened to conceal evidence of their mutual engagement for fear Pettigrew would tap the door and enter to announce dinner was ready to serve.

"Tonight is out of the question," said he, needing his wits on the morrow, his daughters expected at around ten of morning. "As for the morrow, well, who can say how sober I shall be by nightfall."

166

Pursing her lip, she said, "Oh but of course, I must don my black widow's weeds on the morrow. It is all I have to grace the occasion in decent manner."

"And a fetching outfit it is, no doubt."

"If your taste is for black it may catch your eye a little. I had the gown refashioned before departing from India. It was so terribly prim and proper and not me at all."

He could readily visualise a low cut gown with her feminine assets plumped beyond respectability instead of prim lace-covered décolletage. "Be good enough, Lady Vixen, to be prudent in dress on the morrow. I'll not have you flaunting your flesh before the assembled. Constance will go to her resting place with due respect."

"I would not do otherwise nor dishonour her memory," said she, a coy smile, "but our indulgent enjoyment of each other this night will plague your thoughts, and drunk or otherwise on the morrow, you will desire that I to come to your bed."

"You may well be disappointed."

"I wager on paying witness to my attire you will be begging my attention."

"We shall see," said he, determined he would not be begging her to come to him, and instead she would be begging him to pleasure her. He withdrew his pocket-watch, which declared eight on the dot. "Pettigrew is slack this evening."

"I did hear a commotion earlier in the dining hall, and Pettigrew sounded most annoyed. It was something to do with misplaced silver. Candelabras, I believe." A sigh escaped: a despondent sigh as she furthered in heartfelt disappointment. "Thievery it seems is rife today, for I went to the artist's studio to collect my portrait and it was gone: stolen. And would you believe it, the militia were there because the artist had been murdered. Could my luck be

167

any the worse, and then Ranulph Brockenbury, dear fellow, said he would gladly convey my beauty to canvas." Her shoulders sagged in despondent manner. "As much as I would like another portrait, the sittings are such a tiresome business."

He was rather glad the Constable had removed her shredded portrait from the cottage, which had seemed only right and proper at the time. On reflection it did seem sensible to let her think it was stolen, for had she seen its sorry state she would have caused a hullabaloo the Constable could well do without. There was no reason to suppose she was in any danger, the wrath of Harper's killer venting anger merely her misfortune.

"Do you think I should accept Ranulph's offer?"

"It would keep you out of mischief."

He had the measure of the damnably selfish young woman, and while she had free board and lodging under his roof she would oblige his every whim and leave Rupert to pursue his heart's desire. If nothing else their mutual indulgence had finally quelled his hunger for Estelle.

"Dinner must be ready by now." He gestured toward the door. "Shall we?"

"Indeed," said she, a mocking curtsy. "Your Grace is most kind."

"Behave Caroline, or it will be the worse for you should anyone suspect we are intimate in any way, whether by thought or action."

She reached for his hand, drew it to her lips and licked his forefinger, but momentary. "Are you sure you do not wish me come to your bedchamber tonight?"

He opened the door and ushered her into the corridor, a pulse in his nether region declaring he was not as aged as imagined, the years falling away with every step. "Discretion, Caroline, discretion at all times."

Seventeen

Huish Downham.

Constance was laid to rest, and carriages and coaches were departing and friends and family were exchanging heartfelt condolences in keeping with the solemn occasion of the day's proceedings: a kiss to cheek here, a kiss to cheek there. His grace all the while heard mutterings and whispered discourse all around as the sea of faces moved in waves toward and away from him. He shook hands that clasped his in passing. He nodded sagely in response to each and every well wisher; a wave of hand and smile where warranted.

Having indecently imbibed far more wine than was good for keeping a clear head and sharp mind, peoples' actions were slowly drifting into a misty haze, their words canting on the ether as he sidled toward the periphery of those departing from beneath the *porte cochère*. He fancied taking the air, and began walking away from the assembled, his daughters and Rupert more than capable of taking the helm in his absence.

Drawing deep breaths he was glad the need for keeping up appearances would soon be at end, for Constance was at rest in the required stateliness to which she would have approved with a charming smile, albeit feigned in his direction.

In like to Estelle, he wasn't sure he knew what love was anymore. It was so long ago when he and his first wife were wed: he being barely ten years and seven and Anne a little older at ten and nine. It was an arranged marriage admittedly, but a love of sorts had grown out of the union which begot them two daughters. Although it may have been merely a marriage based on familiarity and fondness, it was a short-lived marriage and left with a motherless two-year old and newborn daughter, his father had advised on seeking another wife for the sake of the girls. Along came Constance, whom he had lusted after and her father had been keen to see her wed to a marquis, the match rapidly sanctioned and they were wed within a matter of three months. But it was never the marriage he had imagined it would be, and Rupert became his consolation prize. Although Constance had readily embraced the girls to her heart and reared them as if they were her very own, it was he and Rupert who had lost out.

Mistresses thence came and mistresses went: a string of them and none lasting more than a few months until Estelle tipped the balance of his orderly life. But again, it wasn't romantic love he had felt for Estelle, else the thrill of the pact they had agreed upon, whereby he could look but not touch would have been cast aside and he would have laid the truth before her. And last evening with Caroline in blatant and whorish manner, the vixen baring herself and keening his touch and he weak in giving sway to base need. Dear God he wished he knew whether he could be strong and deny renewed hunger awakened from within should she catch him alone.

He walked onward past the stable mews and circumnavigated his way around to the walled garden backing the mews. The cool touch of metal to hand whilst opening the wrought iron gate brought Caroline's black widow weeds to mind. There were veils aplenty and not one provocative in like to Caroline's. Indeed her assets were shrouded on entering the church by a fur-trimmed pelisse, and face shrouded by fine veil cascading from a miniscule hat perched on her head.

Later, when all were back at the house and Caroline reappeared with her pelisse discarded: her gown was so fine the slightest movement enhanced her contours silhouetting line of thigh and buttocks. Despite her veil utilised as a wrap cast from shoulder to shoulder in modest fashion, her assets although veiled drew the eye. Every time she had stepped into his line of vision his thoughts drifted to their indulgence the evening prior and he would be sore tested in turning her away should she enter his bedchamber after the midnight hour.

He closed the gate and strolled onward past the glasshouses, his duties abandoned in wont of peace and a moment to gather his thoughts. In part he could understand Estelle's desire to return to Hazel Grove, and more than thankful she had sent a letter in the care of his under-coachman.

Her refusal to use the carriage provided for her had surprised him somewhat. It appeared as though she was cutting all communication, unwilling to accept his help in like manner to refusing use of Rupert's carriage.

What hope then was there for Rupert in regaining her trust, as he was wont to do, as he had stated on his return that very morn?

Having witnessed his son in company with Caroline at the funeral service, to all intents and purposes nothing had changed between them. She had appeared as attentive toward him as before and likewise Rupert with her, but he knew his son, knew in his heart Caroline had lost him.

At present Rupert had no idea where Estelle was, but come the morrow he would no doubt ride out and head for Hazel Grove. All any father could do, was pray his son would win the day, and if nothing else it fell to his shoulders to keep the vixen preoccupied whilst Rupert made amends to Estelle.

Increasing his pace he made toward the steps leading to the garden room doors. Once inside he had no alternative but rejoin the family, for Constance' will had yet to be read by Edwin Lord Brockenbury and her wishes carried out as writ.

It was still dark and awakened with a start and unsure of the hour of night, the clock on the mantel chimed one of morn.

He yawned; for three hours of deep sleep was all he had garnered, and he was damned if he could remember having left the candles alight in the candelabra beside the bed.

Sudden movement beside his leg caused his heart to miss a beat. It was all but momentary fear of the unknown until hands slid up his legs and the coverlets rose before his eyes. About to verbally chastise Caroline and dispatch her quick sharp from his room, breath caught in his throat near choking him.

Damn her hide, how dare she ignore his request for her to stay away from his bedchamber until his daughters had vacated the house. He drew breath, his heart palpitating. Her fingers in his groin were deliciously tempting in tease, and such hardness manifested his resistance waned and he wanted her. God forgive him, but he would have to have the naked wench.

About to cast the coverlets aside and sate inner desire to see her naked glory beneath the glow of candle light, her lips embracing his manliness stole his breath, quite stole his senses. He gave sway to the lusciousness of her mouth and tongue savouring his life-force. He was slave to her lips,

172

slave to her fingers, and slave to the heady euphoric haze as he grappled to recover from her sensual onslaught. God give him strength to resist her efforts to render him helpless to the joy of release, for he must, simply must have the pleasure of sheathing himself within her before the ultimate of spent man would leave him breathless and heart pounding.

He slid his fingers through her hair, gripped her head and although half wanting to spend himself and let her have her way with him, his desire for more compelled him to cease her torment. A few moments of intense pleasure and spent bliss were not enough. They had the whole night before them, and he wanted the joy of slow lingering agony and ecstasy. To that aim he reached down between them, hooked his hands under her armpits and hauled her upward. With her cleft felt and entrance sought, in one quicksilver upward thrust he was inside her. He rolled over, taking her with him, pinning her beneath. She was his now to do with as he pleased, and please himself he would and pleasure her as she had said Rupert had never bestowed upon her.

The sheer joy of feeling her clenched about him, her bold embrace of legs wrapped around his torso, his hardness kissing her very core caused madness about him not experienced in a long while. Taking possession of her mouth, his tongue emulating his hardness slithering snakelike within, she responded by thrusting her pelvis to meet his every forward lunge. How foolish to have wanted to cast her aside and send her on her way, when she so willingly and bewitchingly gave her all in stirring his senses.

Aware his ardour could lead him beyond sense of reason and spoil the moment in overspill he let fall her lips from his possession, and said, "Lower your legs, and lie still." She did as bid and he rolled onto his side keeping her sheathed about him. "We have the whole night ahead of us, and I'll not spend until you, Lady Vixen, beg to be released from my bed."

"Then you will be in absolute agony for a long while, your Grace."

"And worth the agony," said he, withdrawing a little, whilst toying a burgeoning nipple between forefinger and thumb, her sighs music to his ears. "I asked you stay away this night, and for your disobedience I am of mind to spank your derriere."

A sensual and tempting chuckle rumbled from the depths of her slender white throat, as his hand landed a sharp spank to mooned flesh.

"I have a little confession," said she, wiggling her hips. 'You see, you please by size alone, for I have not had the pleasure of such a large man before, and I have another confession."

"And that would be?"

"I am so going to miss your magnificent cock," said she, as coarse as a whore in snuggling closer, forcing him deeper whilst at the same time clenching tightly about him. "But you see, dear Lord Brockenbury handed a package in to my hands, and I now have all that I need to take possession of my late husband's estate."

"Ah, I see," said he, savouring the lushness of her heated self gripping him ever tighter as though she feared he would retreat and cast her from his bed.

"No, you cannot see, cannot understand my plight," said she, a hand cupping his face in a dramatically theatrical manner, "for I am torn between the pleasure to be gotten from your bed and that of heather clad heaths and the grey stone walls of my Scottish castle." She faltered, drawing breath, and he sensed his little vixen had something playing on her mind and about to plead a favour from him. "You

174

see, Hubert and I departed for India almost immediately we were wed, and I only have his description of Kelkirky, and I do so wish to explore its vastness. Not only that, I . . ."

Bored by verbal distractions he tweaked her nipple, causing her to lose momentum and derived extreme satisfaction with several mighty thrusts in order to retain his ardour. "I am flattered my ample proportion is so gratifying."

"And I much in regret at having to say farewell to its pleasing properties," said she, pressing closer, no doubt to enhance the sensation of his hardness sheathed within her delectably wanton body. "Would you think it awfully presumptuous if I were to ask a great favour of you?"

He had not expected less. "And this favour would be?"

"Might I have a loan of Constance' carriage?"

"For what purpose?"

"In order to travel to Scotland."

"By all means, dear Vixen," said he, withdrawing his aching mass. "Now cease your chatter, for your tongue is too active, and my tongue thirsts moisture."

She let slip a giggle as he slithered down to nuzzle her silky black muff, his tongue seeking and exploring the softness of her plundered flesh, but still words flowed forth from her. "I shall regret the loss of this delightful treat, as well."

He had nothing more to say for the joy of the moment became heady and intoxicating as she too embraced his hardness with her lips, for mutual indulgence of this nature was wholly new to him. Dear God, she could be the death of him, and he could think of no better way to die than in the throes of orgasmic bliss whilst savouring the delights of her sweetness.

Eighteen

Huish Downham: 6 a.m.

How, how could it be?

She could barely breathe. The callused hand to her throat gripping tight was terrifying. The man's weighty body astride her, holding her down, nothing short of mortifying, and the bearded face before her as alien as the eye patch.

What had happened to him, why only one hazel eye displaying malevolence where once love and devotion had dwelled?

"You filthy whoring bitch," declared Hubert, her not as dead as imagined husband; his voice lowered so as not to rouse the house and dispatching shivers of fear down her spine. "I knew you'd be back here in hope Rantchester was still available and still foolish enough to fall foul to your cock sucking self. You've had no notion that I've been watching you flaunt yourself in the manner of a haughty marchioness, have you? Believe it, Caro, many times I've very nearly sneaked up here to your bedchamber to enact revenge. And I'll have you know I've been plotting this moment, and you'll not escape me. There is to be no happy end to this encounter."

The bitterness in his voice sent a chill shiver down her spine.

"You didn't even have the decency to wait and see if the second round of troops sent to rescue us had succeeded. Well they did and saved three hapless souls besides myself from a fate worse than death." He lowered his brow to her brow, and she could have sworn a tear fell from his eye and splashed against her cheek. "You bitch, why? What did I do wrong?"

Oh God, she had believed him dead and gone and not having cared at all when the news came through that he was reported missing in enemy territory. No, no, she had cared, but not enough. Then it was reported he was dead. If she could tell him she still loved him, it might help to save her from his wrathful anger. She could deny she had only married him to spite Rupert, though it would be a lie.

A heartfelt groan of anguish escaped his lips. "Christ what a fool you made of me in thinking you ever loved me."

If only he would release his grip she might be able to win him over, but that was not to be. He was tightening his hold upon her. Breath failed her and deathly darkness began to embrace and cloak about her, his words chilling as sense of life faded beyond her grasp.

"When I am done here, I shall pay visit to Rantchester's mistress."

There was time, yet, to make amends. Rupert strode from the breakfast room and whilst hastening across the grand hall, Hettie called to him from the gallery, attired in a fine velvet bedchamber robe denoting the early hour of her appearance.

"Is father down, yet?"

"Not as far as I am aware."

His elder half-sister hurried down to stand alongside him her blonde hair bed ruffled, blue eyes darting in all directions in fear of being spied in her bedchamber attire. "Did you hear a scream at around six this morning?"

"Scream, what sort of scream?"

Hettie grimaced, looking a tad thoughtful. "I suppose, on reflection, it was more that of anguished cry than scream."

"If I had I would have investigated its source, but no, I heard nothing."

"How strange, because Drucilla said she heard nothing."

"Perhaps you heard a vixen crossing the park. Its cry would sound much like a woman screaming for help."

"Well yes, I know that, but I am sure I heard a woman's cry. I thought at first it was a maid calling, so I hurried to the bedchamber door. There was no one in the corridor, and darling Digby said I had imagined it. Like you, he heard nothing. In fact my hastening from the bed awakened him from slumber."

Rupert laughed. "Happen you dreamed the scream."

"No, I was wide awake at the time of hearing it, and what is more I swear I heard a door shut in rather a hurried fashion as well."

"In your corridor?"

"Of course, but it was not Drucilla or Archie."

"How is sis, this morning?"

"Oh, much better. I think it was all that standing in church. She is after all, six months with child. Which reminds me, do you think Digby and I should call at Monkton Heights on our way home?"

"It would be a nice gesture, and Georgette will be pleased to see you."

"I should go, for she will soon be with babe to cradle." Hettie drew breath, a smile stealing across her lovely face, very much her mother's face: pretty with a cute button nose and dimple to both cheeks as witnessed from her mother's portrait. "Do you think it might have been Caroline up and about so early of morn?"

"Unlikely," said he, knowing Caroline was anything but an early bird of morn. "I've only known her to rise early on hunt days. Thrill of the chase 'n' all."

"Are you and she . . . how shall I say . . ."

"No. We are not."

Hettie wrinkled her nose. "Oh I see, because Drucilla and I thought, well . . . we thought on seeing you both together yesterday that you had forgiven her for running off with Hubert Somerville. Though why you ever sought her company quite escaped us. She is after all, not one of us. Oh, and that reminds me. Did you happen to see the new groom atop Constance' coach when it returned to the mews, just as we were all setting off for the church?"

"New groom?"

"You are so unobservant, Rupert. Yes, we passed him en route. The one who came seeking a position soon after that young lad Draper disappeared overnight, of whom it was supposed had run off to enlist in the army. I quite thought the new groom in profile was Hubert at first glance, until I noticed his beard and eye patch and that his hair had more grey than black declaring him much older than I had remembered." The door bell clanged: incessantly. "Goodness," exclaimed Hettie, hand to heart, "who would come calling so early? I must look a frightful mess."

"It is now ten after eight, Sis," said he, as Pettigrew appeared from the staff passageway and marched quick-time to answer to the summons from without. "To the male eye you look as though having just tumbled from your husband's lustful embrace."

"Rupert you are shameless in saying such things," said she, drawing her robe tightly about her and not a thought given to the rags still attached to her hair as a means for glorious ringlets to adorn her slender neck.

With the door flung wide Pettigrew allowed entrance to the Constable and captain of the militia, both of whom stepped inside. "Marquis . . . your Ladyship," said the district Constable also a local squire and gentleman of note. His rotund figure as always dutifully attired in the best of cloth and tailored to perfection, his ruddy face was indicative of a man with a penchant for the finest of wines. "Would it be possible to have a quiet word with his grace?"

On the point of summoning Pettigrew to attend upon on his grace and forewarn of the Constable's presence, Rupert decided to do it himself. "Pettigrew, show the Constable and captain to the morning room."

As the men walked away, he chuckled, unable to resist a moment longer in making mention as to why amusement had flickered on the faces of all three men. "You are a sight to behold, Hettie, with your rag bows."

Her hands flew to her head. "Oh no, what must they have thought of my standing here like this?"

"How pretty you look no doubt, in a comical sort of fashion."

A rosy flush flooded her cheeks as they then turned about and made their way up the staircase, she as keen as he to know why the Constable had come to call. "Do you think the Constable has substantial evidence to do with your mother's accident that might lead to an arrest?"

"I doubt it, but he may have information relating to Harper's death."

"Quite possibly, and did you know Caroline's portrait was slashed to ribbons? Daddy let her think it was stolen rather than upset her with the truth."

"Are you sure? If that is so it changes everything. Hell. I remember now."

"Remember what, exactly?" asked Hettie, as they hurried toward their father's bedchamber.

181

"Mother and Caroline swapped horses before setting off from the mews on that fatal day."

"But why?"

"Caroline had begged to ride Nero the night prior. Mother agreed and then changed her mind come the morning of the hunt."

"Oh my . . . Do you think someone meant to do Caroline harm, serious harm?"

"Such may link Harper's murder to mother's tragic death."

"*May*?" squawked Hettie. It must, surely must link everything to Caroline, but why?"

"The sooner his grace goes below the sooner we shall know what it is the Constable has to impart."

Hettie dashed to her bedchamber; saying over her shoulder, "I shall get dressed directly."

He tapped his father's bedchamber door, and summoned to enter, stepped inside.

Surprised at the untidy state of his father's bed and the fact the duke was minus a nightshirt, had it been anyone other than his father in the dishevelled bed he would have looked underneath it in the belief he would find a woman hiding there.

"The Constable is here with a troop of militia."

Looking as though having suffered a restless night, his father boomed in disgruntled voice, "What in the deuce does he want at this hour of the morning?"

"We shall know soon enough. In the meantime, Hettie and I have it in mind my mother's death was neither accidental nor intended."

"It was accidental or it was intended. It cannot be otherwise."

"It seems more than probable the reason the girth had evidence of a slash mark is to do with Caroline."

182

"You are of mind she murdered your mother?" stormed the duke. "Good God, why would she?"

"Quite the opposite, for we think she was the intended victim of harm."

"Damn our sorry hides," exclaimed the duke, "for the Constable and I misread the evidence." Taking no heed of his son's presence in the bedchamber the duke cast aside the coverlets and lunged naked from the bed to grab at a robe. "Send Archer up here," he said, striding toward his dressing-room, "and order Pettigrew to ply the Constable and the captain with wine in copious quantity. I would prefer they depart from here in cheery manner and vague notions of events as shall unfold in meaningful discourse."

"And what of Caroline?"

"Leave her in blissful ignorance for the time being."

About to leave in order to summon his father's valet and set Pettigrew to his given task, he faltered on exit from the bedchamber. "Hettie thought she saw Somerville atop mother's coach on its return to Huish a day past. She was wrong of course for she knows it cannot be him, but nonetheless, it might well be a relative who could gain from Caroline's demise?

"His father reappeared in the doorway of his dressing-room. "Dear God, if that be true, then she is very much in danger here and best we get her away as soon as possible."

"Agreed, and I'm of mind to take a walk around the mews and see this man for myself."

"No, *no* Rupert. Bide time, and we shall arm ourselves and pay visit to the mews with the Constable. No heroics this day, dear boy, unless absolutely necessary." The duke let forth a heartfelt sigh. "Now, see to those tasks, and I shall be down anon."

183

Nineteen

Hazel Grove

Estelle waved Harris on his way.

As the governess cart began trundling along the drive, her personal maid Dora came to her side. "He's a kindly man and better than some gentlemen as I know of hereabouts."

"Indeed Dora. I can never thank the duke's butler enough for his kindness and caring manner."

Dora's fine featured face conveyed sense of concern. "Come away now mistress, for remember what he did say about keeping to the house until the private drag is loaded with your worldly goods and we all ready to take our leave on the morrow."

Estelle turned to look at the property she had hoped might be her home for a little while longer, quite assured the coachman and groom from the private coaching company would see them safe throughout their intended journey. "I shall miss this house."

"It be a pretty house," said Dora, appraising roses adorning its walls amidst the foliage of the Virginia Creeper, "and the creeper is turning redder as the days pass."

Even now Estelle wished she had the courage to stay, but by noon she, Dora, Molly and Parker would be setting off for Devon. She had no idea beyond taking rooms at inns along the way as to where they would end up for sure. It was agreed they would explore the Somerset coastline where possible and have a grand holiday en route. If perchance they came upon a house or heard of one to rent along the way they might consider it, if its location suited their tastes and her means.

A sigh escaped; a heartfelt sigh, for the remainder of the household staff would remain at Hazel Grove until Rupert's generosity ceased to be, and she sincerely hoped all would secure new positions quite easily with a new tenant. She had it in mind to write recommendations noting their individual abilities, of which Parker, dear man, had already taken upon himself to write as soon as her decision to leave was declared.

There was so much to consider, not least the fact she had fled from the duke's house and merely a letter then left in explanation as to why she had brushed aside his kindliness toward her. Wholly convinced her decision was the right course to take she had to look ahead not back at her life as it had been or where it might have led. Love had escaped her grasp more than once in her lifetime and who could say what might be lying in wait to surprise and delight her on her next adventure? It had to be an adventure not merely fearful flight from an unknown entity and flight from pain and heartache.

Dora caught up her hand in girlish manner a big smile. "Come mistress, you've been loitering too long out here in the open."

As they made toward the door the sound of a horse on approach at the canter drew their attention. Luckily Parker stepped forth and Dora hustled her inside, and Parker said, "Close the door and I'll see to the rider, ma'am."

Both she and Dora hastened to the morning-room, both keening sight of who had come to call, but Dora prevented her from stepping close to the window. "No mistress, you stay here. I shall see who it is." Waiting with bated breath,

Dora soon eased her mind. "'Tis just a letter ma'am, a lad have delivered a letter."

She fled the room to see Parker closing the door of which he bolted as soon as it met solid to the doorframe, the letter to hand. "From Monkton Heights is where the lad is from," said he, the sound of the horse departing at the trot audible.

"Did you offer him refreshment?"

"I did, ma'am, but the lad has more than one letter to deliver around the district and was in a mighty big hurry to be on his way."

"Oh, I wonder, I wonder if it's news about the baby?"

With the letter handed over she could not open it fast enough, but it was merely a hastily scrawled missive:

Dear Estelle, you will no doubt be pleased to hear Georgette is well and we were, to our utmost delight, blessed with the presence of a daughter at precisely two of the clock this very morn.

Edwin.

Such glad tidings could not have come at a better moment to lift to her spirits, and its informal presentation implied she was thought of as a close friend rather than mere acquaintance. "A girl, they have a daughter."

Dora clasped her hands together delight etched on her face, her thoughts rapidly revealed. "That is the first smile I've seen in a long while."

As they strolled back into the morning room, Estelle expressed inner happiness. "I am so very pleased for her ladyship. I sincerely believe she secretly wanted a girl on this occasion and Georgette will so love having the companionship of a daughter in the years to come."

"As maybe," said Dora, "and the little miss will never have to lift a finger but a servant will scurry to her summons." Estelle's eyes levelled on Dora, and Dora cast a mischievous smile. "Her ladyship strikes me as one who will spoil the child, and I dare say his lordship will be putty to beauty all over again."

Estelle laughed, for Dora hailed from the ranks of former staff at Hazel Grove before she herself had taken up residence. And Dora had long since revealed much about Georgette and Edwin and their love affair: always in affectionate manner and not the least seedy in tone.

"Mark my words," added Dora, "that child will want for nothing."

A shadow cast across the room and then it was gone as quickly as it appeared. Dora rushed to the window, and then shouted for Parker.

"What did you see?" Estelle's heart began pounding, fear once again gripping her.

"I cannot be sure, but I think one of the men from the coaching company looked in through the window."

Parker appeared at the door. "Is there a problem, ma'am?"

Dora relayed in haste her suspicions and as Parker hurried from the room, Dora said, "Perhaps you should go to the second floor. Molly will be up there packing the trunks by now."

It was an eminently sensible thing to do if strangers were looking through ground floor windows, and she indeed hastened on her way whilst Dora set off after Parker. Upon reaching her bedchamber Estelle found Molly leaning out through an open window, evidently keened to events unfolding outside. She rushed across to join with Molly, the girl quick in moving to one side.

"Sorry ma'am, but I heard Parker accost that man and I wondered what was up because he do sound so very cross."

Estelle refrained from leaning on the sill in like to Molly, but nonetheless well able to see and hear the heated

188

exchange, in which a young man was defending himself in vigorous manner. "I only glanced in the window in passing," said he, sounding vexed at being accused of mean intent. "I meant no harm by it and I ain't a thieving vagabond looking to see what's for the taking of in a hurry."

"The worse it would be for you if that was your intention," said Parker. "Now my lad, you had better have a good reason for skulking round the front of the house poking your nose where you shouldn't."

"I have, and it were me boss the coachman as sent me looking for a buckle."

"A buckle?"

"Aye, a buckle be missing from one of the luggage straps. We have spare straps but we have to account for the broken ones, and if I can find the buckle we can mend it and that way we won't get docked from our pay."

Estelle's heart stopped racing. The young man was innocently trying to prevent himself and the coachman from unnecessary expense. It was a small price to pay for some whilst for them it probably amounted to several pies and a few tankards of ale.

"And your looking in at windows?" challenged Parker.

"It ain't often we do get the chance to see inside the grander part of houses, and . . ."

"All right," said Parker, cutting the young man short, "you can get on with looking for your buckle."

No more was said and while Parker stepped back to the house the young man continued with his search, pacing slowly back and forth across the driveway where her trunk was unloaded the previous evening.

Molly straightened up, eyes still beyond the window and suddenly exclaimed, "Did you see that, ma'am?"

"See what?"

"A man, *there*—" stressed Molly, pointing to the trees in the distance edging the paddocks to the right of the window. "See . . . there he is."

Estelle spied merely a glimpse of dark shadowy figure." Heart in mouth, she sensed, sensed it had to be the man who had murdered Harper. There was no one else she could think of who would be loitering, watching, waiting his chance to enter the house. The only arms at the house amounted to the weapon carried by the young man outside when atop the private drag, though Parker had been known to bag rabbits, pheasants and partridges and was a good shot by all accounts, but he was no match in stature to the man who had murdered Harper.

Dread and fear gripped her and she suddenly could not think, simply could not think straight. Molly on the other hand quick thinking pulled the drapes across the window, and said, "Do you suppose it's the man you were afraid might come here?"

"I think it is, and I know not what we can do to make the house any more secure than it already is."

"No ma'am that is true," said Molly, readjusting her mobcap and smoothing down her apron. "But that young man out there and the coachman might help in keeping you safe from any harm, and I know as how the stable hands will stand side by side with Parker if needs be. We do have guns in the game pantry, and perhaps we could send word to the Constable."

"I cannot see how any rider will get past that man unnoticed."

"No but I could, ma'am. He wouldn't think any consequence to a maid walking past with a basket, and as soon as I reach the pastor's house and tell him what is afoot here, he will surely let me use his gig. I can make it to Bath within the hour if I canter his horse on the flat."

"No Molly, you cannot, must not go out of this house. It is far too dangerous."

"But I must go and tell Parker the man is out there," said Molly rushing for the door. "He has to know."

"We don't know for sure that man is of evil intent. He could be a poacher on his way back from the Duke of Leighdon's estate."

"Better be safe than sorry," said Molly, scurrying through the doorway.

Estelle walked to the window and peeped between the drapes in hope the man had moved on, but no, he was still there. She could not wrench her eyes away and watched him as he in turn watched the house. It seemed an eternity of standing there, and then joy of joys he moved out of sight trailing a horse behind him. She waited awhile to be absolute sure he had indeed gone away. Her heart then dived for he returned and a flash of reflected light implied he was watching the house closely by way of a spyglass.

She let fall the drapes and stepped away from the window, for his action declared he had come prepared and nothing would deter him in his desire to silence her. He was going to wait for nightfall and no one would see him out there in the dark, while inside the house when lit with candles he would see all. From the woodland edge he could take flight so easily if Parker and the stable hands made toward him, armed or otherwise. He would then return perhaps by night alone and no one would know he was there, let alone on approach to the house.

Her heart fell to her feet. Oh how she wished Rupert and she were as one again. That he was there in the bedchamber keeping her safe and reassuring her that all would be well. Alas he was not and instead he was paying court to Caroline.

She turned to the bed sank upon it and tears flooded forth.

Twenty

Huish Downham

About time.

Upon his father's entrance to the library, the Constable and the Captain of Militia hastened to their feet wine glasses to hand, whilst Rupert made toward a window seat.

"I take it your visit at this hour of the day is of some importance," said his grace.

The Constable quick with answer, said, "Indeed, and a sorry time it is in Downham Village this day."

The duke settled his rump to his desk and no hint or gesture afforded to the men to settle back to their former seats, the duke's tone curt. "What has occurred in Downham to dampen the spirits of the villagers?"

"I was given to understand by young David Draper's parents, that he was employed here as a stable hand," said the Constable, in brusque response.

"True," said the duke. "He was a carriage groom to my late wife. The young blighter scarpered overnight and not a word of his going. Is he in some sort of trouble?"

"Young Draper's body was discovered a day past in the copse at the crossroads."

"By God, so he didn't run off to join the army."

The Constable's ruddy face turned grim. "He perished in similar manner to that of Harper. By the same hand it would seem, though such cannot be proved until we catch Harper's killer."

A sharp rap at the door caused a halt to proceedings and Pettigrew's entrance was swift and without due approval from the duke, the man's address informal: "Lady Somerville is in a very bad way. Damn near strangled. Your daughters are with her, and I've sent for the doctor."

As the duke stepped ahead of Pettigrew, the Constable and the Captain of Militia downed their glasses and followed; impeding Rupert's advance. Caroline was obviously alive and it didn't take great intellect to work through Hettie's former remarks about a groom resembling that of Hubert Somerville. The damnable fellow must have survived capture by tribal rebels, returned to England, and had clearly lost his mind. *Why else would he wreck his wife's portrait and attempt to kill her*?

Whilst rushing up the staircase Rupert pondered his mother's death and knew, knew Hubert was responsible for what had happened to the duchess. His beautiful mother had died a tragic death and all because of Hubert enacting some bizarre revenge against Caroline. *What in the name of the devil had Caroline done to turn Hubert from solid soldier to crazed killer? And why did he kill Harper?*

Upon entering Caroline's bedchamber he saw his father's face drain of colour, for Caroline's neck was black and blue, her voice a mere whisper and almost indiscernible, as she struggled to say, "Rupert, you must . . ."

Ignoring his father, she frantically beckoned Rupert forth, her hand thence clasped his tight as she struggled for more words; and barely managed, "Estelle is—"

"She's at Hazel Grove," said his father, concern etched on his face as their eyes met. "An unsealed missive left at Grosvenor House by Estelle was handed to Pettigrew on the return of your mother's carriage to this house, and Somerville no doubt read it en route

Rupert's heart sank for it was a certainty Hubert had gone after Estelle.

Caroline let slip his hand and exhausted by the effort of relaying what she had somehow gleaned from Hubert, she looked to Hettie, who quickly held a glass of tonic water to her lips.

Rupert stepped away from the bed and made fast exit from the room, one thought uppermost. He ran along the corridor to where his sabre once wielded at Waterloo now hung in its scabbard as a reminder of his days as a cavalry officer: his portrait above depicting Rupert Marquis of Rantchester in full military dress alongside a gallant charger.

Snatching the sabre and scabbard from the mounting clips, heart in mouth he hastened onward, his father's voice at his back no consolation. "I'm coming with you."

"We're all going," said the Captain of Militia, following alongside the Constable.

Rupert Marquis of Ranchester needed no one for what he had to do if need dictated, and pray God he could make it to Hazel Grove in time before he lost Estelle forever.

Hazel Grove

Such a brave lass.

Estelle could not believe Molly had wilfully slipped out of the back of the house unseen, but there she was hurrying along the driveway basket to arm.

Parker, as Dora standing beside him, both quite despairing the girl's madness albeit extreme brave of her in seeking help from the pastor.

Watching with bated breath fearing the worst Estelle's heart went out to Molly, for the drive was quite a distance to walk betwixt the house to main gates. Nonetheless the girl was soon passing the parallel line to that where the man was hiding amidst the trees. In fact long before she drew near the man ducked out of sight, and now nowhere to be seen.

Parker and Dora, standing back from the undraped window, keened Molly's every movement just as Estelle could from her hidden vantage point behind the drawn drapes.

Every step taken by the girl added to the tense atmosphere in the room.

Whilst pondering whether Molly had let herself out of the house unassisted, it suddenly occurred to Estelle a door might now be left unbolted. Parker must have thought the very same for he suddenly spun on his heels, and whilst departing the bedchamber, said. "I hope she made sure one of the scullery maids bolted the door after her."

Dora with eyes not leaving the window and that of Molly's fate, said, "Praise be to the *Lord*, she's made it safe to the gates."

Estelle watched Molly turn left and disappear from view, and once again searched the tree-line to the right but there was no man: nothing. "He's disappeared."

"That he has," said Dora, "and which way might he be treading if any?"

"Would he suspect Molly as anything other than a perfectly innocent maid going about her business?"

Dora kept her eyes to the window. "He might wonder at the hurried pace of the girl, though the basket on her arm could well have fooled him in to thinking her departure is of no consequence. It is you he seeks, ma'am, and if he's of a mind to strike a blow in daylight, Molly's departure might have given him false hope of entering a house ill-prepared for the likes of his kind."

196

"I think he must be quite deranged for the way in which he murdered Harper was brutal indeed, not to mention how much poor Harper must have suffered beforehand."

Estelle prayed Molly's exit from the servant's quarters had not left the house vulnerable to attack, and all she could hope was Molly might make it to the Constable or alert the militia to her plight and that of the occupants at Hazel Grove before it was too late.

They'd ridden hard, all the way from Huish to a half mile short of Hazel Grove.

Appreciative of the Constable and the militia at his back, they were, as a troop, about to turn off the highway and onto the lane that led past Hazel Grove, Ranchester was damnably glad he had managed to persuade his father to remain at Huish. Albeit reluctant at first, the duke had conceded armed men were needed to patrol the grounds in close proximity to the house, and it fell to him to issue guns to servants' capable in handling weapons.

No one knew for sure if Hubert Somerville had departed the house and to be absolute sure there was no more threat to Caroline or anyone else in the house it needed searching from top to bottom. He doubted not his father would be barking orders and the household staff rallying to his every demand. The house would have no closet, no dressing room nor secret passageway left to chance of a person hiding within.

Reining back from canter to trot in order to take a sharp left turn his heart began pummelling for they were closing fast on Hazel Grove. With the turn taken alongside a spinney and the horses barely back to trotting pace they were forced to a halt; a pony and gig bearing down on them at a fair licking trot. Rupert wondered if the sturdy pony would slow before ploughing into the militia at his back, but a girl's voice hollering and a good hand on the reins she pulled him up sharp and true.

"Thank the Lord," said she, dark brown eyes levelled on Rupert. "You better get up to the house as quick as ever you can, sir, for there be a man loitering in the woods to the left of the paddocks as you go through the gates. The mistress is right scared."

Turning in the saddle, he addressed the Captain of Militia. "Somerville will hear us on approach if we go in as a troop of horse and we may lose him."

"Aye, true enough," came the response from the Constable, "What say we dismount and fan out through the wood on foot?"

"We won't make it past the gates unheard or unseen," said Rupert, reining Huntsman about. "Instead it'll mean taking a detour over the hill, and coming back through the wood from higher up."

"Then so be it," said the captain reining his horse about, as the troopers and the Constable accepted his knowledge of the immediate terrain would serve them best. "Lead on your lordship."

Rupert led off, Molly wishing him luck.

They were under siege, no doubt about it.

Parker had fetched up a tray to the upper sitting room and Dora was busying with pouring tea for three as ordered by Estelle. She felt it was only fair to share the niceties when they were sharing in her nervousness and her fear and keeping company with her.

Despite a pistol and rifle at hand Parker was not a young man and she feared as much for him as for herself, God forbid they should suddenly find themselves face to face with Harper's killer. To point at game with a gun was quite different than to shoot another human, and she wasn't sure she could point a pistol at anyone. Dora had said *she* could and swore she *'wouldn't miss if that man out there dared to show his face'*.

Nonetheless not one of them had spied the man for almost an hour but they felt sure he was still there, *'biding his time'* as Parker had said, *'and likely as not taking a snooze'* which seemed plausible if his intention was for a night assault upon the house.

With cup and saucer given to his hand Parker kept to his vigil at a discreet distance from the window, Dora as bad and at his elbow. Estelle sipped at her own cup of tea. Normally soothing in times of stress it afforded little comfort as her thoughts drifted to the past few days.

She replaced her cup to tray, despite dryness of mouth and heart pounding, for one fearful encounter with a man unseen but heard treading a destructive path within a portraitist's house had brought her to a pitiful state of not only running from heartache but hiding from someone she didn't even know.

The sudden report of a shot echoing across the valley resonated with impact in the room as the shock of it caused Dora to drop her cup; thus the sound of china shattering adding to their sense of uncertainty. Parker placed his cup safely to the tray, picked up the rifle and moved a little closer to the window, while Dora hastily gathered the pieces of fine bone china and mopped at spilled tea with a table napkin.

"Never mind," reassured Estelle, equal in mopping at the spilled tea, "the gunshot made me jump, too."

"Lordy lordy," said Dora, "I am so sorry, ma'am, I thought I was braver than that, and to think young Molly went out there and walked right past that rogue as though promenading in Milsom Street to catch the eye of a young buck."

"I think I must be seeing things," said Parker, drawing their attention. "No, no, 'tis the red coat of a militiaman coming down the rise on the edge of the woodland on foot."

Dora scrambled to her feet; pieces of bone china chinking inside the gathered napkin now held in hand, likewise Estelle.

"Oh, I see him," exclaimed Dora. "And there— there's another. See him— along the upper edge of the woodland? He's on foot, too."

As Estelle dared to move closer to the window, Parker scratched his head in ponderous manner and said, "Soldiers are out there all right."

"You can be sure it was Molly who told 'em where to look for him," said Dora, "though only God do know how, for 'tis a miracle seeing as how she couldn't have gone a mile in the parson's gig in the time she've been gone from here."

"Then perhaps they were passing through or they were coming here on purpose," intoned Parker, shaking his head in disbelief at Lady Fate having had a hand in the militia alighting on Hazel Grove just when soldiers were needed most.

As yet nothing was certain as the redcoats began closing on the position where the three of them had all witnessed the man standing in the shadow of the trees. Estelle's heart then lurched for a dark bay horse and its rider broke cover by leaping over the fence. At the same moment the militiaman on the lower edge of the woodland raised his weapon, aimed and fired.

The horse and rider continued on a direct path across the meadow toward the driveway, the rider seemingly unperturbed and uninjured.

It was all happening so fast and it seemed likely he was going to evade capture. The trooper's on foot had no hope of detaining him. Then two mounted militiamen on greys appeared followed by a chestnut and man in green. All three horses jumped the fence with ease and soon at the gallop in pursuit of the fleeing man. The rider in green could not be anyone else but Rupert. She recognised Huntsman and Rupert in the saddle. They were as one galloping at speed, his hat having toppled from his head, his golden hair unmistakable.

But with sword drawn as though engaged in a cavalry charge?

Her heart began to race, for the rogue seemed as though reining back a little, his horse dropping to a slow canter on approach to the iron railed fencing edging the paddocks. At that moment one of the pursuing militiamen fired his pistol.

Parker cheered and said, "He got him, I swear he got him in the shoulder."

It did look as though the rider faltered momentarily. Nonetheless the dark bay cleared the railings and just managed to turn on the driveway before heading away from the house and toward the main gates. Rupert suddenly reined Huntsman across the meadow and gained valuable distance on the fugitive, while the militiamen followed the same path as that of the fugitive by way of the fence and onward in pursuit.

Holding her breath in fear of what might happen next, she closed her eyes because she knew, just knew Huntsman was going to leap the fence aslant and thereby gain further ground on the fleeing horse.

A cheer from Parker and scream of delight from Dora implied Rupert had made safe passage over the fence. "By God, they've got him, because if I'm not mistaken that's the Constable with two militiamen barring the gateway."

It was over, she was safe, and every person in the house was safe. She embraced Dora, briefly hugged Parker much to his delight and surprise, and then the report of a gun once again echoed across the valley.

Her heart stalled. Oh God, Rupert. By jumping Huntsman over the fence the way that he had, he would have drawn alongside the fugitive within a few strides. *What good was a blade against a gun?*

She fled the room. Fled the house, and ran and ran and ran until she reached the men and horses standing in a huddle. She hurriedly made her way past the two greys, both troopers having dismounted and one in charge of both horses. The fugitive's horse was in the care of the second militiaman, and her spirits soared on seeing Rupert had dismounted and looking none the worse for his mad dash.

The trooper holding the dark bay, said, "Best go back, Missy, 'tis not a pretty sight."

Now that she knew Rupert had suffered no harm, she had no wish to see what had happened to Harper's killer. She turned about and set off back to the house, her heart at her feet. She should not have come outside, should not have come so close to Rupert. How foolish, for even now after all that had happened she loved him, would always love him.

Hitching up her skirts she ran tears streaming, the path ahead becoming a blur and the sound of a horse pounding the ground at the trot from behind of little consequence until it drew level and circled round cutting off her retreat.

202

"Estelle," said Rupert, sliding from the saddle, "We need to talk."

His closeness and hand laying gentle to her shoulder proved as tortuous in touch as all the times when he had made love to her: it was unbearable, with her confused and he searching her eyes.

Was he seeking forgiveness to ease his conscience?

"I love you. Estelle, as I've loved no other. Your tears are my tears, and my heart is yours for always, no matter what. God knows I did wrong in helping Caroline in financial matters and neglecting your needs, but I had my reasons for keeping her distant from you and all that we had. You had every right to turn your back, and whilst grieving your loss I once again sought the evils of opium and Caroline, damn her hide, encouraged me. Believe me, I have not taken her to my bed nor did I go to hers."

She wanted to believe him, but to put her trust in him would weaken her resolve to leave Hazel Grove and him behind.

More to the point, dare she reveal the extent of her love for him?

The touch of his fingers tilting her chin upward caused her heart to falter. "Estelle, you've always said Huntsman and I are as one when together. Can you and I not be as one . . . for always? Can you not be the one whom Georgette Lady Brockenbury will say tamed The Dark Marquis? For that is what the ladies of the *haut ton* call me."

"And won't they think me foolish for becoming the mistress of The Dark Marquis?"

"As a mistress, perhaps, but as my wife, no. Envy though, will be rife within the midst of the *beau monde* if you step out on my arm. Do you think you could bear that?"

"I could bear it well enough, so long as you stay close."

"I'll not be leaving you alone for a minute if you agree, now, this very instant, to become my wife. For where I go, you go."

Her heart tripped over itself. "Then I accept your proposal."

His lips conveyed all that needed to be said, his embrace offering a permanent cloak of safety. And upon letting slip her lips from his, he caught up her hand and led off, Huntsman faithfully following in their wake. "Were you that worried about my hide," said he, a broad smile, "in your rushing to see for yourself if doom had befallen me?"

"I thought that awful man had shot you."

He chuckled, squeezing her hand in affectionate manner. "I confess I had intended relieving old Hubert Somerville of his head for daring to come after you, and because of what he did to Caroline. Alas, he thwarted my plan by putting his pistol to mouth and squeezing the trigger."

"Caroline's husband? So he wasn't dead after all."

"Dead now, and unlikely to rise again barring a miracle."

"And Caroline?"

"Black and blue about the throat and short on voice after his near choking the life out of her, but I dare say in a few days she'll be making someone's life a living hell. Nevertheless, all thanks to Caroline, we arrived here before harm befell your pretty hide and for that I am truly grateful to her."

As they strolled toward the house she pondered whether he really was *her* Dark Marquis. And yet he had come back to her despite Caroline's every efforts to tempt and lead him astray. She could forgive any indiscretions in his absence for it was she who had banished him from her heart and her hearth, and had he turned to Caroline she could not have laid blame on his shoulders. There were many things to

204

consider, not least the fact he was unaware that her muddled emotions and up and down moods previous to his storming from the house had escaped their notice as anything other than that of a vexed mistress.

Should she tell him the truth before they were wed or afterwards?

Epilogue

Huish Downham: mid-August 1820.

How glorious the day.

Whilst engrossed in gathering lavender stalks; Estelle cursed her negligence at having left her gardening bonnet in the house and no parasol to hand. The sun bearing down on her head and back although wonderful in one sense, her face, neck and arms had already turned honey-gold in her foolishness for discarding clothing rather than shrouding her skin when taking the air.

Goodness knows what her lady friends would say if they could see her. Though Georgette Lady Brockenbury was prone to similar foolhardiness, and oft when strolling across the green to take tea in the pavilion beside the lake her ladyship would cast a parasol aside, thrust her face skyward, twirl around and pay homage to the sun in a wickedly delightful manner.

There was no lake at Huish Downham, admittedly. Instead the formal water gardens were fed by a spring, which served purpose as a pleasant distraction. There were stone seats aplenty in and around the rose garden, and indeed allowed time for sitting and pondering whilst drinking the perfumed air.

She cast a glance at her basket left lying on one of the seats. It had more than sufficient lavender stalks for bundling and hanging to dry in the summerhouse. She straightened her back musing at how on occasion the *little palace* as she referred to the whitewashed summerhouse, had often provided much needed shelter from a passing

207

summer shower. For it overlooked the bowling-green where croquet was played far more than that of bowls and it was a place where she often retired to for afternoon tea.

Yes, there was much about Huish to appreciate inside and outside, and at present she had freedom to wander at will any time of day or evening. How long that privilege would last was anyone's guess, for no one knew when the duke would return from his grand tour, for as yet there was no word of his having reached Venice.

Placing the last of her gathered lavender to the basket along with snips, she proceeded to remove her cotton gloves. To date brief missives from his grace had merely announced departure from one place and that of his next destination, and no mention of whom he had met along the way and no word as to whether he was enjoying himself. Equally, no word had come from Caroline as promised on her departure from Huish. So whether the castle inherited from her late husband had fulfilled her dreams, Rupert nor she were party to.

It was all rather strange for his grace having escorted Caroline to Scotland would no doubt have enlightened them on his return, but no, he had instead returned to London, thus a brief missive to say he had arrived safely in London and would be taking ship to the Continent directly despite it being January and bitter cold. By April his grace was in Vienna unaware that he had a grandson, and until such time as he provided an address to which Rupert could send word, his grace would remain ignorant of the infant who was now four months of age, whom according to Rupert might have reached the grand age of two before Alexander's grandfather showed face at Huish again.

Flushed from the sun bearing down she picked up her basket and hurried to the shade of the summerhouse where Dora had left a jug of lemon and ginger cordial. Glad of the cool shade she settled to an old chaise longue brought there when heavy with child she had longed to escape the main house, the summerhouse perfect to rest mid-stroll through the gardens.

It really had become a favourite retreat where she often whiled an hour or two with a book, a sketch pad or settled to write letters. She could not bear it when Alexander had cried in the early days and had always given sway and picked him up and cuddled him, and his nursemaid had then scolded her and insisted she would rue the day if she always ran to him when he demanded attention. Unable to hear him from the summerhouse, after a day or two he ceased in his demands upon her and equal measures of his wakefulness and sleep soon made for a contented household.

Refreshed with a glass of cordial she kicked off her silk slippers and lay back on the chaise, eyes closed, only to hear, "Estelle, where are you?" boomed from the terrace.

Rupert could jolly well look for her; instead of expecting her to answer to his every call. Goodness, how alike father and son were.

Venice: mid-August 1820.

Duke of Leighdon he was, and consummately happy at last.

With sixty-three years of living a relatively restricted existence tempered by social etiquette, and latterly marital encumbrance lacking in love, the clandestine affairs he had embarked on over the years had rarely fulfilled his needs as expected until now.

No one cared if they were wed or not when he and his new lady love swept into Venice salons and ballrooms in grand manner, nor did anyone raise an eyebrow when it was obvious they had lain abed of an afternoon relishing the delights of sensual bliss. There was no doubting her rapturous cries echoed through the rooms of the waterside house, and his agonised groans in the throes of imminent and gratifying release could be heard by the passing gondoliers.

Anyone and everyone acquainted with her knew she had now become the Duchess of Leighdon that very morning, and whilst showered with flowers thrown from waterside balconies they had kissed and would have made love in the canopied gondola if not for the fact she had wished to be seen and not shrouded by drapes.

She was still given to slumber in post-wedding feast euphoria and of copious quantities of wine, not to mention exhaustion from his ardent physical ministrations as her newly appointed husband and lover. Whilst leaning on the iron railing surrounding the balcony at her bedchamber window, he thanked the Lord she had come to him and loved him as he had never been loved before, for it was true they relished unbridled love in equal measure.

It was time to settle to writing a letter to Rupert, for there was much to tell of his adventure to Scotland and of Caroline's fate, and of the heady nights in Vienna. He reached into his pocket and withdrew the miniature of Estelle, the provocative image thus a reminder of his unabashed attempt to blackmail her to his whims. He had no need for seductive imagery, not now, and it would be unseemly to keep her close at hand. And yet, it was not the easiest of things to let slip the beautiful artwork from his grasp, but he did and watched it plunge to the waters below.

"Mein Leibkling. Ich will Dich lieben," reached him in the now familiar husky Austrian lilt, and thereby stirring his senses beyond reason.

"My pleasure, dear duchess, but you do realise you may yet be the death of me."

"Pah," said she, pouting her luscious lips, "You have yet to show me your home, and we shall make love all the way there and back again."

Dear God, he felt reborn, for the once Countess of Amalfi had a voracious appetite for him in all his rampant glory, and both now having found true love after disastrous marriages. An Austrian fair beauty by birth and Italian widow of means, at fifty-one she was still a beauty in her own right, and if it was her wont to reside in England in summer and Italy in winter, so be it. He was a willing slave to almost her every whim and she vitally slave to one of his.

Kilkenneth Castle: mid-August 1820

Caroline shivered.

It was supposed to be summertime, and instead it was freezing cold. Drawing a velvet fur-trimmed wrap about her shoulders, she cursed the fire in the hearth for it gave forth but meagre spark of warmth to the vastness of the harsh stone structure surrounding her.

In full acceptance that she had no one but herself to blame for her plight of wedlock to a man twice and one half her age, Scotland was most certainly not as she had envisaged, and if she could go back and start all over again she would indeed do so.

She sighed for she was without doubt her own worst enemy. How foolish she had been to slam a bedchamber door in the Duke of Leighdon's face, and all in vain hope of forcing his hand in to making her his wife instead of his mistress. Subsequently, the last she saw of his fine coach and team of four was from the bedchamber window at a wayside inn south of the border. Not a word said nor missive written, he had simply arranged for the private hire of a coach to see her safely delivered to her intended destination. Thence he had set off back to London.

She would never forget her distressed state at finding herself abandoned, and when having proceeded onward into Scotland, Kirkaldy had eluded her despite people telling of its location and pointing the way. Finally and utterly lost in the rugged and unforgiving highland landscape the coachman had said he would drive to the next residence they might encounter, and upon rounding a corner there stood KilKenneth Castle, grand in manner and commanding unhindered view across a magnificent glen.

Oh how elated she was in thinking it was Kirkaldy, until the tall well-built aged laird in residence took pity upon her and told the awful truth that she indeed owned a beautiful little glen not far distant but merely a heap of moss-covered stones where Kirkaldy had once stood. Distraught and floods of tears spilling forth, the gallant laird offered her a bed for the night and with darkness falling fast she had accepted his hospitality out of dire need.

That very night a terrible nightmare of Hubert attempting to strangle the life out caused her to scream out in her sleep. Hearing her screams Hamish Douglas, Laird of KilKenneth had rushed to her aid and ministered to her in a very tender and loving manner. And, whilst keeping company with her in the hope she would again fall to contented slumber he had told her the tragic tale of his first young wife who had died in childbirth, and how uncannily like his young Isobel she was.

His revelations had indeed touched her heart, and unwilling to let sleep embrace for fear Hubert would again

212

pay visit in a nightmare, she had prompted Hamish to know why he had never married again. But he had, and his second poor darling wife had fallen foul to consumption and died within two months of her arrival at KilKenneth. Again her heart had gone out to him, more so on hearing how his third wife had never gotten with child and died from a broken heart in wont of a bairn.

By morning she realised she had indeed fallen asleep and awakened to find Hamish slumbering in a chair beside her bed. Thinking he might catch his death she had thought to slip silently from beneath the covers, and whilst turning to haul a coverlet from the bed with which to afford warmth he awakened with a start and hauled her onto his lap quite convinced she was his first wife Isobel.

It was all very disturbing to begin with for he had kissed her with intense fervour, his hand in exploration and determined to afford extreme pleasure to his imagined lady love. With no escape from the broad expanse of the man or that of his ardour building with intent, she had finally managed to bring him to his senses in pleading her plight with hands forcibly to his chest in attempt to free herself.

A smile strafed her face in the memory of how mortified he was at her nightgown unlaced, a breast exposed, his hand between her legs and substantial manhood announcing its presence. At the time she really had nothing to lose and everything to gain by letting him have his way with her, for she had seen the extent of his wealth. Taking Sir Hamish Douglas to her bed had been little different than tempting Hubert or the Duke of Leighdon, though the latter had escaped her.

And so it was that Hamish her very hairy and white whiskered laird ministered to his and her needs that morning, and by noon a jewelled necklace adorned her throat and little else besides upon her person whilst he adored every inch of her body in ravenous manner. The very next day they had set out for Edinburgh where upon arrival and three days of shopping, he lavished money on the finest of cloth with orders for gowns to be made, her measurements taken, bonnets, boots and slippers purchased.

His proposal of marriage came as no great shock for she had set her mind to that aim. Her acceptance, although teasingly wanton she had implied he might rue the day of wedding her. Undaunted he sought acquisition of a special licence and they were wed within the week. They dined in great style, attended at theatres and danced in grand ballrooms, and for several weeks new gowns were delivered every other day to his town house.

A few weeks before Christmas he insisted they had to be at KilKenneth in time for Hogmanay, and a grand time was had on the promise they would return to Edinburgh come the thaw. But the winter snows fell heavy and stretched almost to spring, and by then it was known she had fallen with child. The laird unwilling to touch her thence forth for fear of damaging the infant within despite her declaring her desires and needs as no less than before, he denied her.

For the moment she had no alternative but to suffer the consequences of a belly beginning to swell, though as yet it was proving no deterrent to a young footman eager to engage in pleasures of the flesh whilst the laird was preoccupied with fishing, shooting and business in Edinburgh. Once the bairn was safely to its cradle she would not then succumb to the master's ardour and become his prisoner for another nine months. Oh no, she had every intention of taking flight from Scotland to London in company with the footman. She had ample monies hidden within a chest and when added to the silverware she intended to filch she would take a let on a house of some standing. It would not be so terrible to become a well-attired *fille de joire* to the upper echelons of the *beau monde* again, and no doubt she would soon acquire status of mistress to a man of substantive wealth.

Pray to heaven the bairn be a boy, for Hamish would be unlikely to follow her trail and pose a problem. After all, he would have that of which he desired most, a son and heir, whilst she then nothing but its mother and of little consequence. He would never know it was another man's child.

She ought really to have written a letter to the Marquis and Marchioness of Rantchester, as promised, but they were undoubtedly very happy and with no interest in what had happened to her. Though she would like to know whether the duke did indeed take ship to the Continent and if he had, it would please her to know his ship had sunk along the way.

The End

If you would like to learn more about me, the author, please feel free to visit my blog https://francinehowarth.blogspot.com.

There you can read articles on historical events, people of note - in their time - who are also featured within my novels, added to which there are personal introductions from the characters.

Thank you; and God bless.

Other books by Francine Howarth

Caveat: Although *Mr. Darcy's Mistress* is a traditional sweet tale with no love scenes, the majority of my books do have explicit sensual or steamy love scenes appropriate to character development and their choices in life. One or two of the books have near rape, and Rape in general is such an emotive subject in today's world, and yet in times past it was a dreadful reality, not least within the imagined safety of the marital home, or in situations of war and retribution. So to set the record straight there are two unbidden molestation/near rape scenes in two novels –Her Favoured Captain and The Earls Captive Bride. However, within my English Civil War Series, book 2 *Toast of Clifton* there is a rape scene, which is motivated by envy and sense of revenge.

To Risk All For Love
A Sinful Countess
In Love with a Portrait
Mr Darcy's Mistress – Elizabeth's Dilemma
The Reluctant Duchess – Regency Murder Mystery
Sequel – The Dissolute Rake
Bath Series – Regency Murder Mysteries:
Infamous Rival –Book 1
The Dark Marquis –Book 2
The Damnable Lady Caroline –Book 3

Family Saga:
The Trevellians' of New-Lyn – Murder Mystery Spanning
the Georgian Period & Regency Era:

~

Venetian Encounter – Georgian Murder Mystery
The Duke's Gypsy – Georgian Murder Mystery.
The Highwayman's Mistress
Celeste
Sequel to Celeste - Highwayman Lord
A Devilish Masquerade
Lady Louise de Winter
The Earl's Captive Bride
Her Favoured Captain
Scandalous Whisper
17th Century Series – Royal Secrets.
Prequel Novella – e-book format – Debt of Honour
By Loyalty Divided - 1
Toast of Clifton - 2
Royal Secrets - 3
Love & Rebellion - 4
Lady of the Tower -Monmouth's Legacy -5

Printed in Great Britain
by Amazon

80456187R00128